I Saw Him Standing There

Holly Kerr

Three Birds Press

1

Day One - Miami

I HAD ONE LEG out the window by the time the banging started at the door.

I knew Eduardo was coming today but I thought I'd have more time. When I first met him, Eduardo used to be known as Fast Eddie. This con, the one he was coming to collect for, was supposed to be the one to bring us to the big leagues.

The problem was, I didn't want to go to the big leagues. And I had no idea how to tell him I hadn't been able to go through with his latest confidence scam. There was nothing for him to collect and a whole lot to clean up after.

I sat on my bedroom window ledge, the cement scratching the backs of my legs, and contemplated my options.

It was only a short swing from the ledge over to the balcony next door, only a short four-story drop if I fell.

The banging inside was getting louder. "Siggy! I know you're in there!"

I winced, tightening my grip on the window frame. Eduardo does not sound happy. He was expecting me to meet him at the door with smiles and a stack of bearer bonds I was supposed to have acquired.

No smiles. No bonds.

Our carefully laid plan had gone horribly, terribly wrong, all because I had been struck by an attack of conscience.

"Siggy! Open the door!"

With a deep breath, I turned on my belly and hung from the ledge by my fingers. Swinging my legs to get enough momentum, I flew across to the other ledge, landing awkwardly with the heavy backpack and my camera bag slung across my chest.

I could lose the backpack, but the camera went everywhere with me.

The jump down onto the neighbouring garage was relatively easy compared to the first part, as was the next drop. Eduardo stuck his head out my bedroom window as I landed easily on the cracked sidewalk.

"I want my money, Siggy!"

"I don't have it," I called up to him.

"You better be on your way to get it."

With a last glance, I took off down the street, Eduardo's bellow of rage following me.

Andy's car was parked around the corner from my apartment. With a quick glance behind me, I popped the lock with the handy bent coat hanger I shoved in my bag for that very reason. With a silent promise to see the car back to Andy, I climbed in and twined the right wires together under the dash. The car roared to life.

I was out of the neighbourhood before Eduardo could huff his way down the street, leaving Surfside behind me with barely a hint of remorse except a sinking feeling in my stomach.

Beaches and palm trees flew by as I drove. I didn't stop until I passed the Lincoln Mall in South Beach.

Once I passed the mall, I deemed it safe to stop and called Andy. "I took your car," I confessed as soon he answered. "I'll get it back to you. I promise."

I heard noises in the background, Andy rummaging in his closet-sized apartment to find his keys. "I didn't take your keys." Another skill I'd learned from Eduardo. There had been talk of me becoming some kind of Baby Driver, like in the movie, but the arrest of one of Eduardo's friends after an easy liquor store heist had put an end to that.

Andy sighed. "What did he do to you?"

When I arrived in Miami four years ago, I was on my way from transforming myself from the empty-headed party girl who let a man get close enough to take advantage of me and my family, to a badass who wouldn't stand for it. I no longer wanted to be Seraphina Park-Smith; daughter, sister, wife. I said goodbye to my old life and became Siggy Smith, using the nickname my brother had given me as a child.

Eduardo had taught me ways to survive and thrive on my own. Quite a few of those skills skirted the lines of legality while some of them were just morally questionable. I went along with it because I'd been mad and looking for a way to get revenge.

Then the desire for revenge faded and I was left with only two things: the realization I'd become someone I didn't like very much; and Eduardo, who liked who I'd become a little too much.

"I thought last night was to be the big score," Andy said when I didn't answer.

"I couldn't do it." There was a tiny nugget of pride that I hadn't gone through with the plan. "There were kids involved. Eduardo's not going to understand."

"No, I daren't say he will. But I get it. You're not that person, my darling. You don't fit in with us, as much as you try."

"You could have told me sooner!"

"I thought you were happy."

Had I been happy learning the ropes to become a con artist? It had been fun at first, but then it started being serious. I found myself out of options when I snipped the family purse strings.

"I don't know where to go," I admitted.

"You could go back to your family," Andy said in a quiet voice. "You know they'll have forgiven you by now."

"I doubt it." The coolness in my voice covered the longing.

"Think about it. And be careful with my car. Send me a text where you end up and I'll come and fetch it."

"Thank you. I'm sorry."

"For what? Not pulling off the scam? I would have been sorrier if you had. Love you, darling. And I'm proud of you. Whatever happens."

Andy had become my family and had been since he found me shivering at the airport three and a half years ago, all my worldly possessions in my bag, dried tears streaking through my makeup. I had been a perfect mark but instead, he took me in and took care of me.

I was glad I hadn't let him down.

I said goodbye and tucked my phone into the cupholder, wondering what to do now. The backdoor of the car opened.

I glanced around in horror, expecting Eduardo, the cops, my father, anyone but a woman. Prada shades covered most of her face, and she held a glittery phone in her hand. With an exasperated huff, she swung a Louis Vuitton carry-on into the backseat. "A little help would be nice."

I could only stare at her. "I'm not a cab."

"You have an Uber sticker on your window."

Darn it. I forgot Andy sidelined as an Uber driver. "But I'm not—this isn't my car." What was I supposed to do, admit I stole the car? "I'm not on duty right now."

"Just drive me to the cruise terminal and you can call it a day." She plunked her handbag on her lap and my gaze lasered in on it. Kate Spade Maise Satchel in hot pink.

My heart hurt for a moment at the sight of the bag. "I like your bag."

"Of course you do. Put my suitcase in the trunk and then drive."

"I can't put it in the trunk. It's—ah—broken." Or unavailable because I had no key.

She lowered her glasses. "What do you mean, broken?" She glanced around Andy's ten-year-old Toyota with a disdainful expression. "What kind of Uber car is this?"

"I mean, not *un*broken. I can't get into it. So you should get another ride."

"Do you have a body in there or something?"

I lowered my own cheap plastic sunglasses and gave her a look. Her eyes widened and I thought she was really going to jump out of the car. Then I relented. "No body. Just broken. I'll put your suitcase in the back seat."

I didn't know why I agreed. Maybe because I didn't have a plan, and I needed one. I couldn't keep driving aimlessly.

"So where to, once you get to the port?" I pulled away from the curb. Miami Port wasn't too far, enough to give me enough time to make a plan. I could head to the bus terminal and—

"It's me."

I thought she was talking to me until I glanced in the mirror and saw her holding her phone to her ear.

"I have to go; it's all booked. No, I'm not looking forward to it. No, I'm sure it's going to be horrible. Seven days at sea with obnoxious strangers. It's going to be hell."

Hell was this drive with the obnoxious stranger in the backseat.

She paused in her conversation and from the scowl on her face, apparently didn't like the response she was getting.

"It's some sort of love cruise. You board, you fall in love, or you stay in love, or something silly like that. Like being on a boat is some sort of magic spell. *It's not.*"

"Turn down the music."

It took her asking—demanding, rather—twice more before I realized she was talking to me.

"Don't you love this song?" The music was a bit loud but that was how I liked to drive.

"No, I really don't and it's difficult enough to have this conversation without Kelly Clarkson blaring in my eardrums."

Some people were not nice. There are all sorts out there—nasty, rude and basically horrible people live in this world. I didn't know why they were like that, but they are and no matter how nice and considerate you are back to them, it really makes no difference.

This woman was like that. I didn't know who she was talking to on the phone but I wish they'd wise up and hang up on her and let me do my Good Samaritan deed in quiet. With Kelly Clarkson blaring in my eardrums.

But you know what they say about no good deed going unpunished.

I was punished from outside the car as well. Traffic was terrible, definitely not helpful when I was running for my life.

I thought about how Eduardo's face puffed up tomato red when he was angry. And I remembered when Jimmy had his knee problem that happened the same time the deal he was doing with Eduardo fell through.

Yep. It was definitely time to get out of Miami.

My mind was foggy with ominous thoughts as I drove towards the port of Miami, the one-sided conversation in the backseat fading into the background. But the chime of her cell got my attention, as did her excited gasp.

"Oh! Peter!"

She sounded so different that I glanced in the rearview mirror to see a woman transformed. She was smiling and when she pulled off her sunglasses, there were actual tears in her eyes. "I'm so glad you called." She *cooed* into the phone like she was talking to a baby.

Or a man.

"Okay. Okay. Okay, okay...yes...okay... Oh, yes!"

I snickered under my breath. Had she forgotten her words?

"Stop the car!"

"We're not at the terminal."

"I said, stop the car. Right now. Here. He'll pick me up."

"Who?" I couldn't help but ask. After all, if I was acting as an Uber driver, then I was responsible for her, wasn't I?

"Peter." She all but sighed.

"Who's Peter?"

"He's *Peter*. Here, stop here. He'll be here soon."

"Should I wait?" If I hadn't turned around, I would have missed the look she gave me. *Of course, you should wait, you moron.*

Even in love, she was still mean.

"Is he going on this cruise with you?" I asked as I pulled over.

"Of course not and now I don't have to go either." She clapped her hands suddenly. Whoever this Peter was certainly put her in a better mood. "I don't have to go!"

"Do you get your money back? I mean, if I'm taking you to the boat, doesn't that mean you're supposed to be getting on it? You can't just not show up for something like that. They may hold the ship for you."

She stared at me. "They won't do that."

"They might." I had no idea if a cruise ship would hold off sailing if a passenger didn't show up but it was fun to play with her.

"They might for me," she agreed. "Here." She rummaged in her Kate Spade and pulled out a slim black leather portfolio. Taking out a handful of papers, she thrust them between the seats. "Take my ticket."

"What? No!"

"I'm not going to use them. You might as well."

"They won't really hold the boat for you. I just made that up."

"You'd be surprised how many people wait for me."

"I can't use your tickets. I mean, really, I can't. They won't let me. Besides, they're in *your* name." A glance at the papers showed her name was Petra Van Brereton.

"Take my passport."

"Are you kidding me?"

She threw it into the front seat. "I'll get another one. You look enough like me that no one will notice. It's always a hassle boarding; you can slip right through. And you'd be doing me a favour. My parents are going to be furious when they find out about Peter. This way we can get married and they'll think I'm still on the cruise and won't even look for me."

I glanced at her picture. Other than both of us having brown hair, we really looked nothing alike.

I started to hand the documents back but then stopped. Eduardo would never find me in the middle of the ocean. And I'd be doing her a favour. I knew all about upsetting parents.

"My uncle is the captain. I'll call him and clear everything. Use my passport to get on, and then everything will be fine."

"I don't know..."

"Seriously, take it. I don't need them. It's a love cruise—"

"Like the *Love Boat*? You know, that television show from the seventies?" I asked. Her expression changed to annoyed confusion. "It must be on Netflix by now."

"I have no idea what you're talking about. Take the tickets. Take my bag. Go on the cruise. Have a nice life."

I took the tickets.

What else was I supposed to do? She wasn't going to use them, and it was better than wasting them.

Petra was too busy kissing the tall, handsome man to notice when I pulled away with her suitcase. The tickets for the cruise lay on the passenger seat.

I promised myself I'd return Petra's passport as soon as I got back.

When I pulled up to the terminal, I saw a big, beautiful boat docked at the pier with crowds of people on deck.

The *Oceanic Aphrodite*.

If this was really some sort of love cruise, at least it had a good name.

2

I FOUND A PARKING space at the far end of the lot and texted Andy to tell him where to pick up his car. I didn't say anything about getting on a boat. I trusted Andy, but putting plans in a text was a sure way to get caught.

Was I really going to pretend to be someone else and get on that boat? Not only was it *wrong* but it was possibly illegal. I stopped myself from jumping into that lake last night, only to find myself wading back in this morning.

As I stared at the boat, I felt myself wavering. Petra's address was on her passport; I could drop her things off and keep driving out of the city.

My phone chirped an incoming text. *Stay there.*

It was from Andy, but was it really? Had he told Eduardo where to find me?

That decided things.

Petra's suitcase was still in the backseat. She left it with me, walked away with nothing, right into the arms of some man. It must have been love.

It was stupid.

How did Petra know he was a good man, that he could be trusted? That he was able and willing to take care of her? That he wouldn't lie and deceive and pretend to be someone he wasn't? That she wouldn't be left with her heart shattered, her life in pieces, all because she made the mistake of falling in love with him?

I half expected her to roar into the parking lot, demanding her tickets back, along with her suitcase. Because of this, I kept looking over my shoulder as I unzipped the case, not taking a moment to appreciate the details and workmanship in the Louis Vuitton. Right on top was a Tommy Bahama halter dress, white with flowers at the hem. Perfect for a cruise. I checked the size on the label.

Perfect for me.

It had been a long time since I'd been on a cruise ship. As a girl, I'd gone on trips with my parents; once a cruise from Barcelona to Athens. Another time we cruised the Caribbean for my grandmother's eightieth birthday.

I pushed those memories resolutely out of my mind as I strode across the parking lot without an ounce of unease on my face.

To play a role, you have to believe in it. I learned that from Andy and from Eduardo. I was no longer Siggy Smith, part-time grifter, up-and-coming con artist. I was Petra Van Brereton, haughty and snobby and full of pretension.

I stood in line, feigning impatience by tapping the toe of my Birkenstock. I had managed to stuff my knapsack into Petra's suitcase since there was no way she would be caught dead carrying a cheap WalMart bag. The line moved slowly forward, and I tried to breathe naturally, look bored, act unconcerned, even though my heart was nearly bouncing out of my chest with fear.

There was a real cutie in front of me, about four feet tall with blond hair and big blue eyes. As if he knew I was watching, he turned and grinned, showing me the missing teeth.

That ended my Petra act. "Are you excited to get on the boat?"

"Yes," he cried loudly. "Why won't they let me take Mr. Feeney?"

"Ah…" He looked about six years old, so I had no idea if Mr. Feeney was a real person. Maybe a favourite stuffed animal…?" Does Mr. Feeney really *want* to go on the boat?"

"Of course." Dramatic eye roll. "He wants to go everywhere with me."

"Of course he does. Well, does he like water?"

"Ferrets don't like water," he shouted gleefully as though he'd made the best joke ever.

I couldn't help but smile at him.

"They really don't," said another voice.

I looked up and saw him standing there—tall and nicely shouldered with dark wavy hair that could handle a cut but looked better without it. I couldn't help but smile at him too.

And then I noticed his sharply pressed blue pants and short-sleeved, white button down. He was one of the ship's officers, complete with name tag and friendly expression.

My smile faded completely when I noticed him checking tickets.

"I'm guessing Mr. Feeney is a ferret?" he asked, handing the tickets back to the boy's parents but looking past them at me.

"I think you guess right." I glanced at the little boy who nodded excitedly. "I'm sure Mr. Feeney wants to be with you, but do you really think he would enjoy being on a boat? What if he gets seasick?"

Huge blue eyes stared at me. "Do you think *I'll* get seasick?"

"Do you like water?"

"I love it. I'm a good swimmer too. I've already passed level seven and that's the one where you learn to dive. I want to dive off the back of the ship!"

"I don't think you should do that," I said automatically, not needing to see the fear in the mother's eyes. "Definitely don't do that. But I bet there are a couple of pools on board that you can practice your dives in."

"Cool!"

"Ready to board, Sam?" the mother asked before turning to me. "Thank—are you all right?"

"I'm fine," I said, smoothing out my grimace. Sam was my little brother's name. "Have a good trip."

"I'll find you on the boat," Sam promised as his mother pulled him away.

"You can show me your diving," I called after him, giving myself a moment before I turned back to the ship's officer. I arranged my face in a suitable Petra expression. "Hello."

His smile was wide and friendly but it was the way his blue eyes looked at me that made my heart skip a beat. "Do you have kids?"

"Do I look like I have kids?" I fake a laugh as I handed him Petra's—my—passport and tickets in the smooth leather folder. His fingers brushed mine with a warning tingle.

"Never can tell. So who do we have here?" As he scanned the tickets, he gave me another grin. "You should have been here earlier to board with the other VIPs. It would have been quicker."

"But then I wouldn't have heard about Mr. Feeney. Please don't look too closely at the passport," I added quickly.

"Bad picture?" He squinted at it, then up at me.

I smiled ruefully. "The opposite. I took the picture just before I went to this big gala, so hair done, make-up perfect." I gave a roll of my eyes. "My girl was so slow, and it took *so* long with every fake eyelash having to be put on individually. Plus, I've cut my hair since then and stopped straightening it."

"It's a good picture," he said, still studying it. "But it is a little different."

"A lot different," I laughed, pushing my curly hair out of my eyes. Did it seem like I was holding my breath? Counting the seconds until he decided I passed the test?

I glanced around as he continued to study the passport. A security guard was escorting a man past the line. I gave the man a double take. "Oh my god!"

He looked up. "Is there a problem?"

"No! Yes! That's Evan Parker!" When he frowned, I leaned closer. "*Evan Parker?* The singer? You know, 'Nothing Like This'? It's all over the radio!"

"Is that really him?" He looked over his shoulder and I fought the urge to make a run for it.

I kept my voice low so Evan wouldn't hear me. Not only would it be super embarrassing to be caught fangirling the singer, but I've met him on more than one occasion and he might recognize me. He was providing a good distraction, but I didn't want to push my luck.

"Wow." He turned back to me, trying to hide the impressed expression on his face. "I guess he's on board."

"Isn't that exciting?"

He handed the passport back to me and I breathed a sigh of relief. "Yes, but as staff, we're not supposed to make a big deal out of them. They're passengers too, wanting to have a good time."

"I'll remember that if I bump into him." Again, something I will avoid at all costs.

"Justin Sheehan was on board last year," he admitted in a low voice. "I met him a few times. That was cool."

"I bet." I hiked my bag over my arm. "I guess I'll be going then."

"Wait." To my horror, he grabbed the passport back and took another look at it, then at me before handing it back. "Have a good trip," he said casually. "Petra."

The name sounded foreign to my ears. "I will. Thank you..." I peered at his nametag. "Will McKay. Nice to meet you."

Will chuckled. "I'm only a lowly assistant cruise director."

"You seem to be a doing a fine job." I forgot all about Petra and gave him a wide Siggy smile.

He held my smile for a beat, another one until he wrenched his gaze to the next passenger in line.

Despite everything that had brought me here, as I boarded the *Oceanic Aphrodite*, something inside me woke up and stretched.

This was going to be a problem.

3

ABOUT AN HOUR LATER, I stood in the middle of my cabin.

"Good job, Petra," I murmured as I surveyed the one-bedroom suite with the extra large balcony. It was on the stern of the ship, which my concierge told me, was a special experience.

Yes, Petra had booked a cabin with concierge service.

"Once you have an aft-balconied cabin, you'll never go back," my concierge Astrid said, her respectful manner diminished by the twinkle in her eye. "The only disadvantage you have to remember is that people up top like to look over the edge at times. And because your balcony is one of the larger ones, I'd suggest no topless sunbathing unless you want an audience."

"I hadn't really planned on it but thanks for the advice."

I heaved a sigh of relief as the door shut behind her. This wasn't what I had planned when I jumped out the window earlier, but it might work. Even if Eduardo found me, what was he supposed to do? It wasn't like I'd actually done anything illegal, so the police wouldn't be involved.

I glanced down at Petra's passport still in my hand. Using it might be a little illegal, but she'd given me permission. The first thing I had to do was to find the room safe and lock up the passport. It wouldn't be good to lose it.

I knew nothing about the woman who gifted me this trip, this escape. She was like some sort of fairy godmother, only I doubted a fairy godmother would wield such an acid tongue.

As I heaved the carryon bag onto the bed to join my camera, I wondered why Petra booked a cabin this big, this luxurious just for her.

Was someone else staying with her?

No—I rechecked the ticket. Single room and she paid extra for it. But was she travelling alone? Did she have friends on board? Friends who would expect to meet up with her? Who might be worried if she didn't show up, and contact someone on the ship, who will tell them, yes, Petra Van Brereton did indeed come aboard?

I should have gotten more information. I should have prepared better.

There was nothing I could do about that now. I began to poke around the cabin, opening drawers and doors. There was a good-sized washroom, a bedroom with a king-sized bed tempting me with every passing moment, and big windows that would give me a beautiful view of the ocean. Right now, I could see the skyline of downtown Miami. The balcony was large enough for a small gathering and since it overlooked the pier, I resisted the urge to stand outside. There'd be time enough for that later. I couldn't wait to get out there with my camera.

There was a sitting room, with a fully stocked mini-fridge, a beautiful fruit basket on the table as well as a bottle of champagne.

I bet they put chocolates on the pillows, as well as the standard towel animals.

I couldn't stop smiling. This might actually work.

And then I heard the commotion in the hallway. Doors banging, shouting, all coming closer to my room on the corner.

He found me.

I rushed to the door and peered through the peephole, waiting with bated breath for Eduardo to reach my door, trying frantically to come up with a plan to get out of this. There was no way I could jump out of the window this time.

Someone was laughing in the hall.

Fists pounded on my door. "Please let me in!"

I peeked through the tiny hole.

It wasn't Eduardo.

There was a shirtless man standing there before my door, tall and dark haired with a worried expression on his face.

I took a chance that he hadn't been sent by Eduardo and opened the door in time to see him sprint down the hall.

Naked.

He was completely naked and definitely not one of Eduardo's henchmen. 'You looking for someone?" I called after him, giddy with relief that he wasn't looking for me.

Nice butt.

He whirled around at the sound of my voice, his hands locked in front of him, but not doing a very good job of covering himself.

"Oh, thank god! You're an angel." I kept my eyes on his face as he ran toward me. "No one will let me in."

"Because you're naked?"

"They think it's funny. They pushed me out when I was changing," he said in an overloud voice, obviously speaking to the unseen pranksters. I heard laughter around the corner. "Can I have a towel?" His hazel eyes had such a desperate quality that I took pity on him.

I also laughed at him. "Sure." I hold the door open for him to dart inside and reward myself for my Good Samaritan deed with a covert glance at his backside. "Maybe you should have one handy next time you decide to get naked." I reached into the washroom for one of the thick towels and handed it to him, this time keeping my eyes on his face.

"Thank you," he said gratefully, wrapping the towel around his waist. "You're a lifesaver."

"I'm always happy to give assistance to naked men."

"Does that happen often?" he asked with a grin.

"No, thank goodness."

He had a very nice smile. "I'd better go and see if they'll let me back in the room. Thanks again." He backed away, still holding my gaze. "You going to that party tonight?"

"I didn't know there was a party."

"There's always a party. Lido deck, ten pm. See you there?"

"Only if you put some clothes on." I opened the door, startling a group in the hall with amazed expressions on their faces. I gave him a push into the hall before giving the group my best Petra look and flash a satisfied smile. "He was magnificent," I said, *a la* Kelly McGillis in *Top Gun*.

After Naked Man left, hopefully, to find clothes, I grabbed my camera and set out to explore the ship. Heading up another floor brought me to the pool deck.

I shaded my eyes, regretting not grabbing my sunglasses. But I held my camera up to my eyes and took a few shots. The colours, the action—kids in constant motion in the pool, splashing and laughing. A waterslide snaked its way down the side of the ship stack and every few moments, deposited a laughing, screaming person into the water.

Not just kids, either.

For a moment I was tempted to rush back to my cabin and change into my bathing suit. Petra's bathing suit. I snapped more pictures and moved on.

There was a party taking place near the end of the ship and as I moved closer I noticed the bride in the white dress. Instinctively, I raised the camera. She was beautiful with dark hair shining in the sunlight and smiling at her groom.

She looked so happy.

My finger stilled and I lowered the camera without taking the picture.

The ship's horn blew loud and long, signalling our departure. A group of laughing girls rushed by towards the end of the boat. I followed them as they joined a large group of waving passengers standing at the rail. The noise was deafening, but the happiness was contagious. I held up my camera and snapped pictures of the group, in high spirits to be leaving Florida behind.

I should be happy too, but I was more relieved than anything. Soon, Miami would be behind us, along with Eduardo.

I aimed the camera at the smaller group on the dock frantically waving. Families saying goodbye to their loved ones—

No.

I lowered the camera for an instant and then raised it again like a shield.

Eduardo was standing on the dock. And Andy was right beside him.

I backed away slowly as to not call attention to myself and more passengers took my spot by the railing, blocking my view.

Numb with shock, I followed a crowd of chattering twentysomethings. My cabin was located at the stern and even though I knew deep down it was safe, I wanted to stay as far away from that side of the ship until the dock, the city and land itself vanished from sight.

I found myself on Deck 6, overlooking the atrium. I caught my breath as I stared below. Once upon a time, I'd been used to luxury and the finer things in life, but the *Oceanic Aphrodite* was something else.

I wanted to see everything at once. I craned my neck to see the levels stacked above me, some with smiling faces looking down. A massive chandelier, almost as big as the one in the Chandelier Bar in Las Vegas, glittered in the sunlight.

Below, a group of staff formed a half circle before a sweeping double stairway, answering questions and directing the passengers. Miles of marble floor was filled with groups of friends and families, all chattering happily, obviously excited to be taking the trip. Shops and restaurants outlined the space, colourful and lively as people explored every nook and cranny of their floating paradise.

A statue of Aphrodite towered over the space, as alone as I was.

The horn blared again and I felt the vibrations of the engines change as the ship raised anchor.

I was really doing this.

A movement from the lounge below caught my eye. It was Will from boarding, waving with a huge smile on his face.

I raised my camera and took his picture.

4

AS WE LEFT MIAMI behind us, I spent a few hours exploring with my camera.

The ship was filled with shiny, happy people; even those green in the face and leaning over the railing were cheerful. Since I'd been living in Miami, I'd noticed Florida had an abundance of happy people, but I thought it was the proximity to Walt Disney World. There was nothing in life that a dose of Mickey Mouse couldn't fix.

But here, with no mouse ears in sight, everyone on board seemed to be having a blast.

I noticed the prevalence of younger passengers. I passed groups that were my age—mid-twenties—or slightly over. I passed three games of pickup beer pong. Every bar had a line-up, and there was quite a bit of horseplay around the pools. I made a mental note to look up the *Oceanic Aphrodite* when I got back to my room to find out if it was some kind of spring break party boat.

But I had no desire to return to my room.

There were maps and directions posted everywhere, which was a good thing because the boat was huge. When I was nine, my parents booked us on a cruise to celebrate my grandmother's eightieth birthday. The only things I remembered about it was that my mother was terrified I would get lost and refused to let me out of her sight for the first three days, that I could eat ice cream any time of the day, and that my grandfather spent half of the trip sick in his room.

I seemed to recall my grandmother having more fun without him.

As I stepped out onto Deck 14, another memory hit me, that of my little brother Sam and my father missing the tender back to the ship when we went ashore in St. Lucia.

That was a different ship, a different time, because my father had chartered a helicopter to bring them back to the ship, to Sam's delight.

I stopped by the boutiques and wandered through the casino. I found the library and curled up with the latest edition of *People Like Us* magazine. I checked out the disco and the lounge, and the six restaurants, becoming hungrier with each menu I looked at.

I had no idea what Petra signed up for, whether it was assigned seating in the dining room or one of the more casual, pick-your-own places. With my luck, she probably had a standing invitation to the captain's table. I decided to miss dinner until I had more information.

Missing dinner didn't mean I wouldn't eat. I stopped for ice cream. I took a mojito and a plate of nachos to a lounge chair on the lido deck and sat in the sun, out of reach of the pool and people watched.

I took pictures of everything.

The light was beautiful, especially when the sun began to dip lower in the sky. The waves danced along the boat, the calls of the seagulls grew fainter the farther we pushed away from Miami.

This might work.

Petra got me away from Eduardo's wrath, but so far there was no out-of-the-frying-pan, into-the-fire thing happening which had been a bit of a trend for me.

I had come to Miami three and a half years ago, after trying to lose myself first in New York and then Atlanta. Both places had too many acquaintances who knew my face and were more than ready to ask about things I didn't want to talk about. Miami was better because as long as I stayed away from South Beach, it was easy to blend in.

I stayed with Andy for six weeks before I met Eduardo and he took me under his wing. I told him nothing about my life, not even my real name. I was Siggy Smith. Seraphina Park-Smith was tucked away, not to be disturbed.

It was fun at first as Eduardo helped bring my confidence back as he taught me how to survive on the streets. It wasn't until it was too late that I realized he was molding me into a criminal, focusing on petty crimes until he felt I was ready for something bigger.

Eduardo taught me how to be a con artist.

I wasn't a very good one. The first time I managed to scam a very sweet man out of his paycheque. I then left an envelope in his door with the exact amount I'd taken. The time after that, I convinced a naïve eighteen-year-old to pay an exorbitant amount of money for headshots for a modelling career. I actually submitted her picture and got her a job in a campaign for Gap. The time after that—

My moral compass didn't like me being a con artist.

Unfortunately, I couldn't tell Eduardo how I felt because by then he no longer saw me as a pet project but as a source of income. I'd been planning on leaving Miami for months before he came up with the plan to get his hands on the bearer bonds. Since then, as if he knew of my plans, he had people watch me.

And now he couldn't touch me.

I sat on my chair until the light faded and it was difficult to see faces in the dimness. I vaguely recalled Naked Man telling me about a party, but that was the last thing I needed to do. Instead, I head for Deck 12 and the closest bar.

Parnassus. There was definitely a Greek-gods theme going on here.

When the bartender turned around, I realized it wasn't just the names that were taken from the gods. His nametag said Adonis from Crete, Greece, and that was exactly who he looked like.

"I loved Crete," I blurted out. "It was so beautiful."

"It is beautiful, especially the sunsets." His smile looked like a toothpaste advert. "What can I get you this lovely evening?"

For a second I opened my mouth to ask for a pint of whatever was on tap, my go-to drink for the past four years.

I'm on a cruise and it's all paid for.

"Gin martini, straight up, stirred, not shaken and with two olives. Hendricks, please." The request rolled off my tongue like I said it every day.

"The lady knows what she likes." Adonis' smile was blinding and contagious.

"The lady hasn't had a martini in a very long time," I admitted.

Adonis' smile grew wider. "Then let's make it a double."

I watched him mix my drink, conscious of the group of women at the end of the bar practically swooning every time Adonis gave them a glance.

"Your drink, my lady."

"Thank you." I took a sip, and then another. When was the last time I ordered a martini? When was the last time I could afford one?

"What brings you to our ship?" Adonis asked, slowly wiping the counter.

A free ticket? "I thought a cruise looked like a fun thing to do," I said instead.

"But this cruise, the *Oceanic Aphrodite*... this is the cruise where Cupid is most at work."

"There's a guy named Cupid?"

"It's called the ship of love."

I reined in the snort. "I think it should be called the ship of naps, or the ship of really good martinis." I held up my glass. "Much more beneficial to me than love."

"Ah." Adonis narrowed his piercing blue eyes. "A skeptic."

"A realist," I corrected.

He laughed and out of the corner of my eye, I saw one of the group of girls clutch her chest. I inclined my head towards them and leaned forward. "I think they believe your spiel."

"Just wait." Adonis smiled over my shoulder. I turned to see a woman approaching the bar. Like me, she was alone, and like me, she looked a little freaked out to be here. At least that was what I expected to look like, had I bothered to glance in a mirror.

"What can I get you?" Adonis asked.

"A mojito, please," she said with a glance at me. "Although that looks good." Her accent was Australian, the words sounding musical to my ears.

"I have to say it's a little potent." I took another sip. "But very tasty. I think this is my new favourite place on board."

She jerked her chin towards Adonis. "I agree. I've been all over this ship today and I haven't seen anyone look like him."

I smiled and she continued. "Not that I should be noticing things like that. I'm here in a professional capacity as a nurse—" She stopped as Adonis slid her mojito, icy and minty with a pineapple affixed to the rim of the glass. "Thanks. You don't want to hear my story."

"It's probably more interesting than mine."

"I'm, uh, helping a client complete her drug rehab on-board."

Drug rehab on board a cruise with free alcohol? I raise an eyebrow. "How's that going?"

"It's okay. Hey," she said in a rush, like she was trying to change the subject. "Did you know half the people on here are part of a singles cruise?"

I motioned to Adonis, now serving the group of chest clutchers at the end of the bar. "He said something about Cupid at work, but I had no idea. This was a...a last-minute decision," I said vaguely, praying she wouldn't ask for more.

"I'm Nina, by the way."

"Siggy."

She narrowed her eyes. "I've never met a Siggy."

"As far as I know, I'm the only one. It's a nickname. My brother had trouble with Seraphina."

I bite my tongue as my name slipped out. I blamed the gin.

"That's pretty, but you look more like a Siggy, especially with the hair." She gestured to my curls, which were so tangled by the wind that I doubted I'd be able to pull a comb through them. "My full name is Olivia, but I've always felt more like a Liv."

"I like it." I plucked an olive out of my martini and popped it in my mouth. "So—you say you're working, but do you wish you were part of the singles cruise?"

"Oh no. Definitely not. I just came out of a relationship and it didn't end well."

I stare into the depths of my martini. "Didn't we all."

That was all the prompting Nina needed. She told me details about her boyfriend, finishing with how he emptied her bank account.

"I never thought he'd *steal* from me," she said, draining her glass. Without either of us asking, two more drinks found their way before us.

"There has to be a way you can get the money back."

"I don't know if there is. I just hope karma comes back to bite him on the ass."

If I had become the protégé that Eduardo had thought I'd become, I could have come up with a revenge plan for Nina. But nothing popped into my head, except memories of my own that I didn't feel like sharing. Telling her my name was bad enough. Charles was the last person who I wanted to talk about or think about. The martini *must* be going to my head.

Nina sucked on the straw with a gloomy expression on her face. "And now we're both stuck on a cruise with all these singles? That's the last place either of us should be." She finished her drink. "I should probably go. Sorry."

"No worries. Maybe we'll run into each other again."

"Maybe we will." After thanking Adonis, Nina rushed off and I was alone again.

5

ADONIS SMILED AT ME. "You made a friend."

"I made a friend." The conversation with Nina had helped me feel less alone.

"It'll be easy to find the love of your life now."

I shook my head and slid off my stool. "Thanks for the drink."

"Enjoy. Come see me again when Cupid's arrow hits its mark."

"Well, now, don't say that, because then I won't be able to come back for another one of these yummy martinis." I took another sip, the gin hitting my stomach in a delightful slither. "But before I finish this one, where's a good place to get something to eat? Not one of the dining rooms."

Adonis pointed to the stern of the ship. "Mount Othyrus is open, but Hestia makes the best pizza." He kissed his fingers. "You might need a glass of wine to go with it."

What the heck? I am on a cruise, and on a cruise, anything goes. "A glass of wine would be lovely."

Taking my half-drunk martini and a glass of 2000 Barolo, I thanked Adonis again. One of the women from the end of the bar looked over and I gave her a wink. "He's all yours."

Adonis was right about one thing—the pizza at Hestia was to die for. I finished up two slices, the martini and my wine, sitting in a corner of the deck by myself.

It was a beautiful night, with a clear sky and the moon hanging low. I'd gotten used to the rocking of the ship, and years of sailing had made me immune to seasickness. For a moment I let myself wonder about Petra.

I hope she was happy with Peter.

After I finished my dinner, I found the stairs and headed up to the next deck. Half of it was the fitness area, where a few brave souls circled the track, presumably walking off their dinner. The other end of the deck was where the action was. Music and laughter, the clink of glasses—I'd found the party Naked Man told me about.

I headed to the rail instead. Lifting my camera, I focused on the moonlight reflecting off the waves.

If I could ignore the noise, it'd be very peaceful.

It wasn't that I was opposed to having fun, it was just that it had been a long time since I'd had any.

Once upon a time, I used to frequent the bars and clubs of Dallas with the best of them. My girls and I had a standing reservation at Theory Nightclub for Thursday nights and took frequent trips around the country when we heard of a new club opening. I'd been a party girl, a socialite, one of those girls who dropped a thousand dollars a night without batting a fake eyelash.

And then I met Charles and everything changed.

A movement among the waves caught my attention and I focused on the darker shapes splashing among the waves. Could that be—

"Dolphins," I said aloud, clicking a dozen shots.

"I've seen them a few times." The voice beside me was so sudden that I jumped, banging my hip against the railing.

"Jesus! Don't do that!" Lowering my camera, I turned with another curse on my lips to find the officer from check-in, the one who had waved from the deck below. "Oh. Captain Will, isn't it?"

"You know I'm not the captain." He smiled and his bright blue eyes crinkled at the corners.

I returned his smile. "Yes, but it sounds nice doesn't it? Assistant Cruise Director Will is a bit of a mouthful for me." I tapped on his nametag. "Why doesn't yours say where you're from?"

"There's not enough room. And you're...Petra, right?" Will laughed apologetically. "I actually called out to you, but you were so intent on the dolphins that you up and ignored me. I thought I got the name wrong."

My heart sank. "I was in my own little world. Didn't hear a thing."

"You must have been because I'm not that good at sneaking." Will stood beside me and gripped the railing. "Where are the dolphins?"

"There." I pointed in the direction, before holding up my camera. "It's easier to see them through here." I still had the strap around my neck and it pulled me close enough for me to bang my head on his shoulder. "Still attached," I squeaked.

"Sorry." He gave me a sideways glance and a shy smile that made my insides roll over like one of the waves. He held the viewfinder against his eye.

He smelled salty, like the sea. And a bit like lemongrass.

"I see them...so cool." Will peered through the lens for a long moment, and I hovered next to him, trying not to touch. Finally, he lowered the camera. "This is a nice camera. Are you a photographer?"

"Not really. Just for fun."

He handed it back. "Really? Because that's a much nicer camera than our staff photographer uses."

It was a Nikon D750—a nice camera, but nothing like the D850 I left back in Dallas. A flick of my thumb turned it off and I let it hang from the strap around my neck. "My grandmother gave it to me. She said I needed a hobby."

"It's a pretty nice hobby."

We stood quietly for a moment watching the waves until I realized that unless I said something, Will was going to walk away and leave me by myself. And for whatever reason, that felt like the worst thing that could happen.

"What's your hobby?" My voice was bright and cheery, unlike my usual voice. It was my social small-talk voice, used whenever my father had wanted me to make an impression.

It was practically creaking with disuse.

Will's forehead furrowed. "I guess I don't really have one. I used to like to draw comics when I was a kid, but I don't do much of that these days."

"I like comic book movies." I cringed at how fake I sounded and to cover, held up the camera to snap a picture.

"Did you just take my picture?" Will asked doubtfully.

"You're very photogenic."

"Can I see?" The strap around my neck forced me into close proximity once again and I held my breath so he wouldn't think I was trying to smell him.

Which I *was* trying to do.

"Looks good," Will admitted. "I usually hate to have my picture taken. And I get countless passengers asking for it, especially on the last day."

"I can imagine." Especially the ladies wanting to have a memento of him. He was very cute with his dark hair. It was so thick and wavy that my fingers itched to run through it.

Why did I want to touch his hair?

"I didn't see you at the party."

"I—no. I didn't feel like a party," I stammered. If Will didn't see me, did that mean he had been looking?

"Don't like parties?"

I laughed softly. "I think my mingling and small talk is out of practice. Was it good?"

He gestured to the bow of the boat. "It's still going on. The Sassy Singles always have a welcome party the first night. It usually goes on for a while."

"What are the Sassy Singles?" I had a picture of white-haired grandmothers doing a jive with their walkers.

"You know this is a singles' cruise, don't you? Or, the love cruise. It depends on whether you believe the legend or just want to meet someone."

I had no idea about any legend and didn't particularly want to meet anyone. "Ah. I'm here by myself, but hadn't really thought of meeting anyone."

"You met me," Will said lightly.

"I did. And Adonis the bartender."

Why would I say that? My social small-talk voice wasn't the only thing that was unused. Any flirting skills I once had seemed to be long forgotten.

"Adonis." Was it my imagination or did Will shift away from me ever so slightly? "So what are you looking forward to seeing on the cruise?" he asked in a polite voice.

"Um..." For the first time, I realized I had no idea where this boat was headed. "Well, this was a bit of a last-minute decision so I haven't had much time to do my research on the ports...excursions..."

Did I have excursions? From past cruises, I remembered my parents booking trips to the various islands.

"Go see Dunn's River Falls in Ocho Rios. And Sting Ray Bay in Grand Cayman is amazing unless you want to go diving. There's a lot to see in Cozumel too, but the cenotes are my favourite."

Jamaica, Cayman, Mexico. At least I know where we're headed.

"Do you get to go?" I asked. "I would hope you'd get to see some of the places you visit."

"The staff takes turns on their days off. This time I get Cozumel. It's a great way to see the world, meet people." Another smile.

It was almost like I could hear the *twang* of Cupid's arrow. Oh no.

6

Day Two - At Sea

I OPENED MY EYES the next morning to bright sunshine because I had forgot to pull the curtains before crawling into bed. Even with the bright sunlight targeting my sleepy eyes, I had to admit that this was one of the most restful sleeps I've had in years. As I smoothed my hand over the cool sheets, I could see many naps in my future.

But not now. I crawled out of bed, making my way to the window. Waves and blue sky had replaced the shoreline. Miami was far behind us.

That lifted a load off my shoulders.

Petra's suitcase had arrived in the cabin yesterday but I had gone straight to bed after chatting with Will and hadn't bothered to unpack. I took a moment to search through the Louis Vuitton for something to wear, laying the carefully folded clothes on the bed to put away later.

As I headed up to the pool deck, seagulls swooped and soared after the boat, their cries disappearing among the sounds of laughter. I followed the excited screams of children to find another pod of dolphins on the port side of the ship.

They were close enough to hear the splash as they played in the waves.

It was impossible not to be happy here.

I woke up yesterday morning in another world—a dark and dingy apartment with water stains on the ceiling, wondering how I was supposed to get out of the biggest mess of my life, and now I was in the middle of an ocean.

With dolphins.

With camera in hand and a smile on my face, I wandered up to the top deck to find a crowd of people, mostly younger women. "What's going on?" I asked a woman who was jumping up and down in the throes of excitement that was a little too much for that early hour of the morning.

"*Evan Parker!*" she screeched into my ear.

"He's been filming his new video since sunrise," her friend supplied in a voice that didn't damage my eardrums. "We tried to meet him, but it's impossible to get any closer."

"Too bad." Even if Evan Parker did remember me, what were the chances he'd see me in this crowd? But I still turned away from the girls.

"Hang on, can you take our picture?"

I blinked back into the present as the girl's voice broke into my thoughts. Automatically I lifted my camera as they quickly posed with bright smiles and their arms around each other. "Over here," I suggested, moving them away from the group and snapped a dozen pictures.

"I meant with my phone," the blond said as I lowered my camera. She handed me her phone with a sheepish smile. "You look like you know how to take pictures."

"I guess." Taking her phone, I snapped a bunch, suggesting different poses and places where the light was better. They were into it, and laughed throughout, pretending to be models.

"Thank you so much!" the dark-haired one enthused. "That was so much fun."

"I want to see the ones you took of us," the blond said. I held up the camera but the sunlight was too bright to see clearly. "We were just going to get breakfast," she said. "Come with us."

"Don't you want to go to the Sassy Singles photo shoot?" her friend asked.

She shook her blonde head with more vehemence than I expected. "That group scares me. Plus look at how I'm dressed." She plucked at the tunic-style top she wore over shorts. "The other girls will be in bikinis and little dresses. I can't pull that off."

"You look great," her friend said loyally and I added my agreement.

"Let's just go get some breakfast. That's Lily and I'm Heidi."

"I'm Siggy." I followed them to the Mount Orynth dining room, a few decks below.

"The worst thing about this boat is that there is so much food," Heidi complained good-naturedly as we slowly filed along the buffet, the aromas making my mouth water.

"I was thinking that was a good thing." I piled eggs and sausages and bacon onto my plate, becoming hungrier the more bacon I added.

"Wait until the waffle station," Lily said. "All-you-can-eat waffles are never a good thing."

"So have you meant anyone yet?" Heidi asked as we sat down, leaning forward with the straw from her morning piña colada caught between her teeth.

"I met you."

Lily laughed. "She meant, have you met a *man*. It's the sole purpose of this cruise."

Will's comments and Adonis' words from last night came back to me. "I heard something about this being a love cruise or something?"

Lily rolled her eyes. "Or something. The *Oceanic Aphrodite* is famous for being the boat that Prince Benedikt of Liechtenstein fell in love with his wife three years ago. He proposed on their last night on the ship."

"I've never heard of him. Or them. Or this boat, really."

"Don't you ever read *People Like Us* magazine? It was all over that—pictures and stories of them, and other couples who had fallen in love. The cruise started getting super popular after that. It's really hard to get a reservation. We've been waiting over a year."

And Petra just threw her tickets at me.

"So what's supposed to happen on board? Cupids fly around shooting arrows?"

"I don't know but there's been more couples meeting on this boat than any others. The story—or legend, whatever you believe in—is that you're supposed to meet your soul mate within twenty-four hours of coming aboard."

My thoughts flashed to Will. "I did meet someone," I hedged. "But he works here, so that won't count. Isn't there some sort of rule? Staff can't hook up with passengers?"

Lily shook her head excitedly. "Not on this boat. Usual rules don't apply, except with the entertainment staff. They're off limits, which is really too bad because I saw this one dancer yesterday who was *hot*."

"There's a group here called the Sassy Singles, but from what I've seen, they're treating this like some *Bachelor in Paradise* show. I'm not into that," Heidi said.

"Me neither. I don't really believe in fate or destiny." I shoveled a mouthful of eggs into my mouth and nearly fell off my chair at how good they were. I haven't had a breakfast this good since I was home and Carmelia—

I pulled myself out of the painful memory with difficulty. "What about married couples and families?" I ask Heidi. "I've seen a lot of them. They shouldn't be looking for their true love if they're already married."

Heidi sniffed. "Not everyone believes the legend."

"I do," Lily said. "People also come to reconfirm their love or reconnect. I love the idea. I really want to meet my Prince Charming. It's so hard being single with bad first dates and silly swiping on Tindr."

"But relationships don't always work out," I argued. "You can't expect to meet someone and instantly fall in love with him. How will you know if you can trust him? That he won't hurt you?"

"You have to trust. That's the scary part about falling in love," Lily said.

"Have you ever been in love?" Heidi asked.

"Once." I toyed with the remains of egg on my plate. "At least I thought I was."

"What happened?"

"Obviously not something good," Lily said. "That's why you're here. To try again."

"That's definitely why I'm here," I lied.

Even with their views of romance differing from mine, I liked talking with Lily and Heidi. I was surprised that I didn't run for cover after breakfast, but instead joined them for a morning mimosa. I even agreed to try out a dance class.

7

"POLE DANCING?" I ASKED in horror.

A woman sauntered across the front of the room wearing nothing with her impressive five-inch heels except her underwear. Unless you counted the feather boa and tiara. Which I didn't.

I nervously stood beside a pole stretching from floor to ceiling. Mirrors lined the room reflecting every angle of myself. There were at least a dozen students, and one man lurking at the back.

Beside me, Heidi grimaced at her reflection.

"I can't believe I'm doing this?" I whispered to her.

Lily took the pole on the other side of Heidi and glanced over at us. "This'll be great," she said with excitement.

"Good morning, everyone! My name is Janey." The woman at the front of the room made eye contact with each of us before continuing her spiel. "This is where most pole fitness instructors will talk about how they're not strippers. I'm not going to do that. I used to be a stripper, and that's how I became damn good at working the pole."

I widened my eyes at Lily, who giggled. "This is going to be so much fun."

Janey continued. "Look, I'm not here to sugarcoat things, I'm here to teach you how to pole. I like dancing. I liked stripping; it paid well. I wasn't putting myself through law school or medical school or raising a bunch of sick orphans. It's just that I like to eat and stripping gave me the money to do that. I'm not ashamed of it."

When Janey said that, it was like a spotlight sizzled on in my head. For the first time, I felt like someone might understand my reason for working with Eduardo. I had been broke, in a strange city, and had no friends. He took me under his wing and tried to teach me something. In his strange way, Eduardo had thought he was helping me.

And I had made the best out of a bad situation, just like Janey. Of course, I couldn't see how stripping would ever be a viable career option, but I didn't know what her life was like. My grandmother used to tell me you shouldn't judge someone unless you walked a mile in their shoes. Looking at Janey's feet, I knew I couldn't make it even a block wearing the heels she had on her feet.

"This class is about getting in touch with your inner self." I watched in awe as Janey swung around the pole. Her body was curvy but strong, with visible muscle tone in her arms and indents in her stomach. There was no way this woman could be anything but sexy.

"Pole means something different to everyone. Some people use it to earn a living like I did. Like I still do, as a teacher rather than a performer. Some people like the confidence the pole gives them." When she got to the word "confidence," Janey jumped up, locking her thighs. With the same seamless motion, she fell backwards, provoking a gasp from Heidi. She spread her arms wide, holding herself aloft by only her ankles.

"Some like to build their strength," Janey continued, pulling herself up and gripping the pole with her hands. She lifted her legs straight out to one side like a flag blowing in the wind.

It was very impressive.

"And some women want to learn to be sexy." She dropped to the floor, glancing at the class with a pouty face.

At the word sexy, Heidi's face fell beside me. "I can't do that."

"Of course you can," I said quickly.

"But I'm not sexy. I'll look stupid."

While Heidi might be considered a few pounds overweight by today's standards, if you looked up the word sexy in the dictionary, there would be a picture of her wearing her little shorts and T-shirt. Plus, she was giving me hair envy with her long, blonde and naturally wavy locks hanging down her back.

I opened my mouth to tell Heidi to look in the mirror when Janey looked over. "That's BS," Janey said. "What's your name?"

"Heidi."

"Well, Heidi, you have signed up for the sexy class. All of you have. Everyone can be sexy, once they give themselves permission to try. When you leave here, you will feel like the sexiest, fiercest bitch who ever walked a deck."

Heidi still looked dubious.

"That reminds me—it's time to put on your shoes if you've got 'em," Janey continued. "If not, there are spare pairs in the back of the room. Don't worry, I clean them after every class."

"It'll be fun," I assured Heidi as we picked out shoes—mile-high stripper shoes of purple and red, loaded with glitter and sequins.

I wasn't sure why I was encouraging Heidi; it was clear Lily was into it so I wouldn't be alone if Heidi decided to bail.

I wasn't even sure why *I* wanted to try this so badly.

Pole dancing was something that the old Siggy would have tried.

Then it hit me—for the past four years, I haven't been myself.

I had always been loud and outgoing, constantly surrounded by friends and ordering my brothers around like some army sergeant. And then I met Charles.

I told myself it had been because I loved him. I stopped hanging out with my friends, tempering my natural exuberance when we were together to give Charles a chance to tell me more about himself.

I stopped being fun, fearless Siggy. And then after he left, I had been hurt, heartbroken Siggy. Angry Siggy. Guilty, ashamed Siggy.

When I met Eduardo, I held on to the anger for such a long time.

But today, as I happily swung around the pole, I realized it was the first day in a long time that I'd let go of the anger and the guilt. Fun, fearless, *sexy* Siggy poked her head out to visit, and I was very glad to see her.

I liked her better.

After the class, Janey stopped us as we were leaving. "How was that?"

Heidi hadn't stopped smiling since she hoisted herself up on the pole, kicking her purple shoes like a little kid. "So much fun!"

"You did great," Janey praised before narrowing her eyes at me. "You're a dancer?"

I started at the question. "In another life." Dance classes had been a prerequisite since I was three years old, progressing from simple ballet to jazz and even hip-hop and acro.

I hadn't danced since Charles.

"You're good. You should come back for another lesson."

"Maybe," I said, feeling my cheeks heating from the praise. "Thanks for this one."

I said goodbye to Heidi and Lily and promised to meet up with them later. They headed off to find the loves of their lives.

I headed off to—

I had nothing to do. It was a heady experience, almost as good as the buzz I felt from the dancing.

After I showered and changed into another one of Petra's outfits—a cute flared skirt and cropped tank top, I headed back to the lido deck. My muscles ached from throwing myself around and my walk was a little stiffer, but I'd been alone so much in the last few years that having other people around sounded like a good idea.

Of course, the first person I saw was Will.

He didn't notice me. I hovered at the railing of the pool deck and watched as he talked to a group of thirtysomethings. The breeze ruffled his curls and his arms were tanned a golden brown.

Lily's words from this morning whispered in my mind, about finding your perfect match on board. I watched Will smiling and laughing.

Was he my perfect match? My soulmate? For an instant I let myself yearn for something I knew was impossible.

Resolve stiffened my spine. Soft words and strong arms came with a price, and the cost I'd already paid had been too high. I pushed myself off the railing. There could no such thing as a perfect soulmate.

Will threw his head back and laughed at something one of his admirers said. Soulmates, my foot. Even though part of me wished Will would look over and see me, I turned my back on the entire idea and walked away.

8

I'D ACCOMPLISHED QUITE A bit this morning, and it was still early. I needed to be caffeinated in order to make it to lunch without a nap.

From the map in the hallway, I found the Athena Java coffee bar on Deck 14.

"What can I get you?" The voice was deep and Scottish and I had to look up—way up—to find a ruddy face covered in a reddish beard.

Instinctively I took a step back.

He looked like a Highlander from season one of *Outlander*. He looked like one of the scary *Sons of Anarchy* bikers.

He looked like Hagrid.

"I, um…" Glancing up, I was faced with a menu. I'd been drinking plain coffee since I got to Miami, but the truth was that I really didn't like it much. But being hard-on-her-luck Siggy meant not splurging on tasty treats.

"I'll make what ye like, even if it's no on the menu," Hagrid said with an accent as thick as a bowl of porridge.

My stomach did a summersault of delight when I spied the extensive list of frappuccino's on the menu. "How about an iced salted caramel mocha crème frappuccino?"

"Comin' ri' oop."

I stood off to the side. He moved gracefully for a man his size.

"Best on the ship," he said when he caught me watching. His name tag read Rueben, from Linlithgow, Scotland.

"I've been there," I said. "To Linlithgow."

"Have ye now?"

"I wanted to visit the castle. I used read everything I could find about Mary, Queen of Scots and when I found out she was born there, I made my parents take me. I think I was twelve. Beautiful place. All of Scotland is beautiful."

"That it 'tis." He set my drink on the counter, heavy with whipped cream and a healthy drizzle of caramel. I sighed happily as I reached for it.

"What makes a Scottish guy work on an American cruise ship?" I leaned in to take a sip from the straw

"What brought you on such a ship?" he asked in return.

"I'm hiding," I said without thinking.

"Who're ye hidin' from?"

I thought for a moment. "Pretty much everyone."

"Me mam didnae want me to come to America. She's what you call protective like so many mams are. I've been always the shy sort, not one for making friends easily. She said I was better off working the land because of me size. But I never wanted that, always wanted to see the world. There was no sense of me hiding out in little Linlithgow just to make Mam happy, as much as I might love her, and I tole her as much. I didnae want to be afraid of what was out there just because I didnae like to talk to people."

"You don't seem to have a problem talking to me."

Rueben's smile edged out from behind his beard. "Because I stopped hiding. Good things happen when you come out from behind the curtain."

By the time I made it to Deck 5 and watched the rehearsal for the talent show on the main stage, I had thought a lot about Rueben's words as I finished my coffee. Instead of getting another coffee, I stopped at a bar near the concierge station and ordered a strawberry daiquiri.

I was on a cruise, after all, and even though it was barely eleven o'clock in the morning here, it was 5 p.m. somewhere in the world.

Then it was back to my room, for once not to hide, but to do some research.

There was a complimentary iPad next to my bed, and I took it and my drink to my balcony and settled in. A sense of serenity settled over me as I gazed at the water. I always loved the ocean and some of my best memories of my father where when he taught me to sail.

Then loneliness crept in. Not one person knew where I was, except Petra, and she didn't care. I didn't exist for once I'd done her the favour of helping her escape by taking her ticket. Who was my mysterious benefactor, anyway?

I Googled Petra Van Brereton.

Facebook, Instagram. She had over five hundred thousand Twitter followers. Daddy dearest was Emeril Van Brereton, a well-known financier from Miami, which made Petra local and would make returning her things easy.

Her Instagram was full of heart emojis. Petra&Peter4evr. So happy! So glad to have found you.

According to the pictures, it was the real deal with Petra and Peter. *Wedding deets coming soon!* I scrolled through pictures of Peter (cute, but looked pretentious in his button down and khakis), the ring (impressive princess cut, at least two karats), Petra's social smile (thankfully no duck lips, but the obligatory forced dimple), and a perfect French manicure shown off against a Venti Starbucks cup.

Deep into the feed, I found something about me. UberGirl, have fun on the love cruise! Would expect an invite to the wedding, but can't imagine I'd go.

Well, then. My first impression of Petra was right on. I shook my head. What a bitch.

No, what a generous bitch.

I unfolded the cruise brochure and took out her—my—itinerary she gave me with the tickets.

We were docking in Jamaica tomorrow and Petra had booked excursions to Dunne's River Falls, as well as a rum cruise. I had dinner reservations at the Mount Olympus Dining Room tonight.

Sounded like fun. It didn't mean I had to go.

Last night had been dinner at the captain's table. I breathed a sigh of relief that I slept through that. I remember Petra telling me the captain was her uncle, and I hoped she had called him to clear things up.

Next, I Googled *Oceanic Aphrodite*.

I found out the cruise line had won awards like Best Premium Boutique Cruise Line, and there was a nice write up about it in *TravelFood* online magazine. Apparently, there were tons of stuff to do on board, like rum tasting, belly dancing, and an onboard library, not to mention a movie theatre, a disco, and a spa where they wrapped you in fresh seaweed and dunked you in exfoliating bubbles.

Pole dancing class fit right in.

Karaoke, open mic nights, afternoon bingo and a bowling alley. Theatre shows, a *Newlywed Show*-type game show, as well as a *Bachelor/Proposal*-like contest.

I searched the website.

Being aboard the Oceanic Aphrodite will reignite your passions as you experience the magic of faraway places that you have only dreamed about. Discover new ways of looking at the world as you travel to the far corners of the globe. Savour your time with imaginative tours and culinary and cultural traditions.

Fall in love.

Legend has it that everyone who boards the Aphrodite finds their true love.

Find your passion on the Oceanic Aphrodite. Our flagship is world-renowned for the luxurious settings. The perfect settings for weddings, anniversaries and to fall in love.

Further searching found pages of stories about the famous and non-famous who found love aboard the *Aphrodite*. I read about Prince Benedikt of Liechtenstein, singer Justin Sheehan's assistant, well-known hotel magnet Elliot Marshall, who fell in love with one of the dancers, and race car driver Declan Dodd, who had his second wedding on board last year.

Maybe there was something to the stories.

Except love was the last thing I was looking for.

9

A FTER MY RESEARCH, IT was time for a nap.

When I woke up, I put a serious dent in the fruit basket and unpacked Petra's clothes before spending a couple of hours curled up on a lounge chair with her copy of Michelle Obama's book.

The seating for the late dinner was at eight thirty at the Mount Olympus restaurant. I debated all day whether to go. I was going to be seated with Petra's friends and my stomach was queasy with the thought of meeting them. On one hand, I was pretending to be Petra, so why would I go to be with people who knew her? On the other, maybe they were worried about her.

The chance of that was slim since I'd been in the cabin for a good part of the day and no one had shown up looking for her.

No one had come looking for me either, which was a good thing.

Finally, when the sun dropped low in the sky, I decided to go for dinner. The grumbling of hunger pains in my stomach cinched the deal.

I took some care with my appearance. Hair straightened to fall below my shoulders. In Petra's bag, I found enough make-up still in the plastic wrappings to outfit a small SEPHORA and I had fun shadowing and highlighting, something I hadn't had the time or the supplies to do for a long time.

Then I went through Petra's clothes. Dresses hung neatly in the closet, all with matching shoes and accessories in little satin bags.

And that was just her evening wear. The suitcase was so big I could have curled up inside and pulled the zipper. Everything had been packed so perfectly that there were enough clothes for a three-week cruise, and I'd never have to wear the same thing twice.

The well-known designer labels made me nostalgic and as I touched the fabrics, I couldn't help remembering when I had a wardrobe like Petra's.

I still had a bit of time before I needed to be in the dining room, so I headed up to Deck 14 for a predinner drink, walking carefully up the stairs in a pair of Jimmy Choo wedge sandals.

I barely stepped out of the stairwell when I heard a familiar voice. "Petra!"

"This is becoming a habit," I called with a smile as I walked towards Will leaning against the Parnassus bar.

"You going to the bar or bumping into me?" Will asked, his eyes never leaving mine.

"Both, I guess." I fought the urge to press my hand against my stomach to stem the butterflies that took flight at the sight of Will. He was dressed in his uniform, the blue shirt fitted to suggest muscles hidden beneath it, with his curly hair wind-blown from a day outside. His blue eyes were bright against his tanned face.

Was that a second arrow from Cupid that I felt?

No. Just...no.

Adonis had my martini poured by the time I walked the short distance. "Your drink, my lady," he said as he added the second olive. "You look lovely tonight."

"You really do," Will agreed. "You look a little more like your passport photo with your hair like that."

The butterflies took flight as my stomach sank. He still thought I was Petra Van Brereton.

Of course he did. Everyone on the boat thought I was Petra Van Brereton. Almost. I searched my memory. How many times had I slipped up? Had I told Adonis my real name?

As this flew through my mind, Adonis moved off to take another drink order. I motioned to the empty counter before Will. "Where's your drink?"

"My boss frowns on drinking on the job."

"Then why are you hanging out a bar?"

"You mentioned Adonis yesterday so I thought there might be a chance that you'd show up here tonight," Will said, shocking me into silence with his words.

"You...here? You came here looking for me?" I stammered.

Will's smile vanished. "Was that not a good thing to do?"

"No...*no*, no, it's fine. A good thing." I couldn't hide the giddiness bubbling up.

His smile was quick to return. "I thought we could look for some more dolphins." Will's blue eyes twinkled and I clutched at the bar in case my knees weakened further. He was cute and nice and had come looking for me. The *no* in my head faded to a whisper.

"But you look like you're headed for the dining room," he added.

"I do have a reservation," I admitted.

"I wouldn't want you to miss that. Scotty H is one of the best chefs in the cruise line and he's making his famous chicken tonight. Maybe we could hang out tomorrow after your excursion. Where are you going?"

"I have no idea." My mind was racing and I would have difficulty telling anyone either of my names right now if they asked me. "Don't you have to work?"

"I'm on duty from seven to four, and then I get a break until the nightly entertainment."

"You spent your break looking for me?"

"Don't sound so surprised. Of course, I wouldn't have to troll the bars if I knew more about you." He raised his eyebrows expectantly.

"Maybe we could get to know each other more tomorrow," I suggested, trying to sort out my thoughts.

Maybe I could tell him who I really was.

Will stayed with me while I drank my martini as slowly as I could until he suggested I go to dinner since the rest of my table wouldn't be served until I was there. Then he insisted on walking me to Mount Olympus.

The dining room was enclosed with frosted windows offering privacy to those eating. "Enjoy your dinner." Will seemed as reluctant to end our time as I did.

"Enjoy yours," I echoed. "Wherever you eat."

"Not in there," he said ruefully. "Off limits for the staff."

"Are there a lot of places on board that are off limits?"

Will leaned toward me and brushed his arm against my shoulder. "Luckily, the passengers aren't. At least, as long as you're not working for Max. He doesn't like the entertainment to associate with the passengers. He's old-fashioned like that. And kind of a jerk," he whispered.

"Do you often associate with the passengers?" I held my breath waiting for his answer.

"Never," Will said with enough embarrassment that I knew he was telling the truth. In the last few years, I'd gotten good at telling when men were lying. "Can't you tell that I don't know what I'm doing?" he continued with a wide smile. "I see dolphins every day but that was the only thing I could think of as an excuse to talk to you."

"You don't need an excuse," I said in a soft voice.

10

I T WASN'T UNTIL WILL left me at the door to Mount Olympus dining room, that I remembered who I was meeting.

Petra's friends. People who knew Petra. People who probably wouldn't be happy to see me.

For a moment, I was tempted to run after Will.

But then I straighten my back and smoothed the skirt of the red Michael Kors sheath dress. I might be as nervous as if I were meeting the gods, but I could do this.

This would be a breeze for old Siggy. New Siggy was letting her nerves get the better of her.

I stepped inside.

"How are you this evening?" The maître'd at the door was a wizened older man with a cheerful smile, and so tiny that even at five foot five, I towered over him.

"I'm good, thanks," I said before clearing my throat. He gave me a knowing look as my voice cracked.

"Are you meeting someone, my dear?" The tag on his pristine white shirt read Mickey from Davao, Philippines.

I'd always wanted to go to the Philippines.

"I'm meeting people and I don't know any of them," I confessed in a rush. "Friends of a friend— sort of. And I'm never nervous. But tonight... " I trailed off with a rueful shrug. "Maybe a little."

Mickey smiled and glanced around. "Wait right here."

I stared after him with bewilderment, wondering what I was supposed to do if another diner showed up behind me. But he was back in a moment with a glass of champagne in his hand. "For you." He bowed as he passed me the glass. "Liquid luck."

"I need it." I smiled as I took a sip. Bubbles slide down my throat as I drained half the glass. "Thanks."

"I hate seeing a pretty girl like you scared of anything. In my experience, nothing works better than a pretty dress and a glass of champagne. And you already have the dress."

"Thank you," I said again, gratefully.

He nodded. "Ready to give it a go?"

I finished the glass and handed it back to him. "Ready as I'll ever be."

I gave him my cabin number and Mickey collared Robbie the waiter to show me the way. I approached the round table of attractive twentysomethings dressed in the latest fashion according to Petra. They were talking and laughing, clinking glasses and no one looked up at my approach. I waved the waiter away before he could pull out the one empty chair.

I took a deep breath. "Hi, there."

No one turned. I hadn't had a more unwelcoming reception since I tried to sit at Cristal Adamson's lunch table in grade six.

"I'm a friend of Petra's," I said loudly. "Not exactly a friend but—"

Heads turned in a flash towards me.

"Petra!"

"Where is she?"

"What happened to her?"

"Did she miss the boat?"

Accusing voices accosted me, mixed with affronted faces, like it was my fault Petra wasn't there. "She, ah, she gave me her tickets. I'm here in her place."

Dead silence greeted my words. Then—"Seraphina Park-Smith? Siggy? Is that you?"

He stood up, towering over the others at the table. My past rushed towards me as I stared at the boy—the man—who used to be as close to a brother was to me.

It took me two tries to say his name. "Miles."

"What are you doing here?" His chair scraped as he stood up. "I haven't seen you in years. Not since your wedding." Miles pulled me into a hug and I breathed in the scents of home—starched cotton, expensive aftershave and the fruity tang of good red wine. "What are you doing here? How do you know Petra?"

"It's kind of a long story."

"Well, you'll need to tell it. Sit—Xander, will you switch with Siggy?"

"What if I want to sit by this Sigalicious?" the redhead mock grumbled as he changed seats, leaving the empty one beside Miles.

"Next time. I haven't seen this girl in years." Miles' smile was blinding, perfect after years of orthodontics. I wished I could return the smile but seeing Miles—seeing someone from home, made me feel like the boat was crashing over a tsunami-sized wave.

"What happened to Petra?" The question came as I sat down beside Miles, from a blonde across the table. She was practically identical to the girl beside her.

They were the only females out of the four at the table who looked remotely welcoming.

"I'm not sure, but she's okay. She gave me her tickets," I said. "It was really great of her; I needed to get away—"

"Man trouble?" The blonde clone clucked sympathetically.

"You could say that."

"Like Charles?" Miles' voice was harsh and my stomach dropped, thinking that anger was directed towards me.

"Not exactly," I said in a quiet voice.

Miles muttered a curse, but then his expression cleared as he squeezed my hand. "Never mind. It's good to see you. It's been a long time."

"And how long *has* it been?" The question was from the women in the seat next to Miles. She was practically a clone of Petra—same thick shiny dark hair and perfect make-up, same haughty expression.

"Four years," I said in a quiet voice, wishing I could slide away from the table and sink through the floor. I shouldn't have bothered with this. No one came looking for Petra so why would they care why she wasn't on board? I knew what these kinds of people were like. I knew what they cared about and what they valued.

But I knew Miles and he was nothing like that, so maybe I should give them a chance.

"Tell me what you've been up to," Miles began. "The last thing I heard..." He trailed off and I saw in his eyes that he remembered exactly what the last thing he heard about me was.

That my husband, the love of my life, the man I brought into my family against my parents' wishes, turned out to be a criminal.

Charles had been a first-rate con artist, better than me, better than Eduardo. Charles had seen me, empty-headed, party-girl Siggy, as an easy mark to get at my family's fortune.

And it had worked—Charles got away with my trust fund, as well as a healthy chunk of my parents' savings after I convinced them to invest in his startup.

Once I found out who he really was and what he'd done, I disappeared. I couldn't deal with the guilt and my family's disappointment. I haven't been home since.

"What happened with Petra?" Miles asked when I didn't reply. He picked up the bottle of wine and poured me a healthy glass. "Let's start with that instead."

I took a gulp of wine, and then another before replying. "Well, I met her when she jumped into my car, thinking it was an Uber. She convinced me to drive her to the cruise terminal."

"But she's not here. She's not on the ship," the first blonde said.

"No. On the way here, she got a call and insisted I pull over. She said she wasn't going on the cruise and gave me her tickets and boarding pass—everything."

"But you can't just change the name like that," the brunette across the table pointed out.

I shrugged. "How do you all know her?" I asked instead. Some of the expressions thawed. A few, like the redhead, probably because of the now-empty beer glass.

"Petra, and Greer, here—" Miles touched the arm of the glowering woman beside him, "—went to school together. It's Greer's thirtieth birthday on Friday."

"Happy almost birthday," I said automatically.

"Gillian—" Miles continued, pointing to the brunette, "is Greer's roommate. Or *was* her roommate?"

"Soon to be past tense," Gillian said, holding up her hand, so I could see the diamond twinkling in the lights of the dining room chandeliers.

"I'm going to have to put up with her now," the man beside her groaned.

"I don't think it's going to be much of a hardship," Miles said with a smile at Gillian. "That's Ari. And that's Xander, beside him." Xander was the redhead with the beer. "He and I were roommates back in the day. And he's Greer's big brother."

"Aren't I lucky?" Greer muttered.

"And last but not least, this is Alicia and Amy."

I nodded at the blondes across the table. I would never be able to remember who was whom. They weren't twins but could pass for it as each gave me a friendly smile, which was more than I could say for Greer.

"So, none of us really knows Petra," Amy or Alicia said as she held up her glass. "Welcome."

And just like that, I understood that they didn't really care whether Petra was there or not. Another weight lifted from my shoulders.

"Well, she told me to tell you—I guess, *you*." I looked toward Greer's sullen expression. "That she got a better offer; that she no longer needs Aphrodite's luck. And something about Peter—"

"Peter?" Greer grimaced. "Does she really think it's going to work out with him?"

"Well, he got down on one knee to propose, so I guess she does." I took more enjoyment from Greer's discomfort at the news then I should. "They didn't notice when I drove away. I even honked. Much too busy to notice."

"Good for her," Miles said. "Well, one mystery solved."

"What's the other mystery?" Xander asked.

"Who's buying the wine tonight?"

11

I NEVER FOUND OUT who was buying the wine, but it wasn't me, even though I drank my fair share as I struggled to get past the awkwardness of dinner with strangers.

And Miles.

"So you've heard about the legend of Aphrodite?" Amy asked as the plates were cleared away. At least I think it was Amy.

"That she's the goddess of love, associated with beauty, pleasure and procreation?" I replied carefully.

"That's she's a boat and everyone who comes aboard are supposed to find their true love," Alicia retorted.

"I've heard that, but I'm not sure if I believe it," I said as I tried to vanquish the image of Will dancing before my eyes.

"Greer does," Amy said in a low voice. I glanced over to see Greer with her hand on Miles' arm, who laughed at something Ari had said.

I lowered my voice. "Are they together?"

Both blonde heads shook the negative. "Not for lack of trying on her part."

"Miles is a great guy," I admitted.

"We're here because it's Greer's birthday," Amy began.

"And she always gets what she wants," Alicia finished.

"And she wants Miles. Greer thinks the infamous legend of Aphrodite would be the perfect way to get him," Amy said.

I glanced over at Miles still talking to Gillian and Ari, even though Greer was patting his arm like a dog wanting attention. "I see it's working out pretty well for her," I said, not hiding my smirk.

After dessert, after finishing off yet another bottle of wine—that was nine for anyone counting, plus Xander's beer, whiskey shot and now brandy. He was going to be feeling it in the morning—talk began about hitting the nightly show.

"I think I'll pass," I said quickly when Amy turned to me expectantly. "I caught some of it last night when I was wandering around."

Which was a lie, but no one had to know that. I made it through dinner and had more fun than I expected. I didn't want to press my luck.

"I'll probably have an early night," I added, hating that I sounded like what my father used to call a fuddy-duddy— a person who couldn't hold up their end of a conversation or wasn't able to socialize properly.

"Why don't I walk you back to your cabin?" Miles offered. "We can catch up. I'll meet up with the rest of you later, okay?"

From Greer's expression, she did not think that was okay.

"Are you going on the excursion with us tomorrow?" Gillian asked.

"Ochos Rios? The zip line?"

"We leave at eight o'clock," Amy said.

I paused for a moment and glanced at Miles, who smiled hopefully. "I'll be there," I promised.

As happy as I was to see Miles, it was uncomfortable to walk off with him, especially with Greer's death glare lasering into my back. I did it anyway, mainly because I knew it bothered her. She might be a good person, but I doubted it.

Then again, Petra was nothing but a witch to me until she passed over her trip tickets.

We headed up to Deck 14, where shadowy figures once again circled the track. Miles had been friends with my older brother. Our families had been close and Miles had been a fixture around our house and at holiday parties and special occasions. He was always nice to me, which was why I felt myself relax as we stood by the port railing.

It didn't stop me from glancing around to see if Will was in sight.

"So what happened to you?" Miles wasted no time in beginning the interrogation, or the "catching up" as he called it.

I sighed, draping my arms over the railing. "That's a much longer story than how I met Petra. And I'm not really sure I want to tell it."

"I heard that Charles wasn't all that he seemed."

"You can say that again." I stared down into the water. "Do you know that if someone falls overboard, they send an emergency broadcast over the ship? But they don't say someone fell—or jumped. They say, Oscar. So if you ever hear Oscar Oscar Oscar, you'll know what's going on."

"And you know this why? Are you planning on jumping overboard?"

"No. Just a fun fact."

"I remember you used to be full of fun facts. Bet your parents are proud."

"I don't remember the last time I made my parents proud," I said quietly. "That's why I left. I couldn't handle the disappointment in their eyes. They blamed me for Charles."

"But it wasn't your fault."

"I was in love with him. I should have known what he was like."

"That's bullshit, Siggy. You know," he mused aloud. "I always liked Siggy better. It suits you. Seraphina is a pretty name, but reminds me of an angel, someone delicate and breakable. That's not you."

"Not anymore, no. After what Charles did to me and my family, I promised myself I'd never be breakable again."

I turned, feeling Miles' gaze on me. "You're different," he said. "I know it's been a while, but you've changed. How long has it been since you've seen your parents?"

"A few years."

"You should get in touch with them."

"I send them a Christmas card every year so they know I'm alive."

"Do you have any idea how much they've looked for you? They were frantic, Siggy. Your mother took a leave from congress—"

"Another thing I need to feel guilty about."

"There's nothing for you to feel guilty about. *You* did nothing wrong."

I didn't know if it was Miles saying it or some magic from the boat, but for the first time, I started to believe it.

12

Day Three - Ocho Rios, Jamaica

THE NEXT MORNING, I spent so much time leaning over my balcony watching the ship pull into port and marveling how the captain could maneuver such a huge ship that I nearly missed breakfast.

Maybe it was having Miles there, or maybe it was because I was docked in a different country, far away from Eduardo, but for the first time, I felt excitement buzzing through me. *Thank you, Petra, you are my fairy godmother*, I thought as I scarfed down my eggs and rushed out to meet Miles and the others.

Xander took charge as we disembarked from the ship. I had a feeling he'd been the one who insisted on this excursion. Everyone was in good spirits as we walked away from the dock to the catamaran that waited to take us to Dunn's River waterfall, a short distance around away.

I didn't bring my camera with me, for fear it would get damaged but it was painful not taking pictures of the clear tropical water and white sand beaches.

As the boat whizzed us along the shore, I pushed my wind-blown hair out of my face so I could stare at the resorts nestled within the jungle.

"It's so beautiful," I said in awe.

"This is nothing," Xander scoffed. "Wait until we get to the waterfall." We sat in a close huddle near the bow of the boat, with the wind sending a spray of water against my bare arms.

"You've been to Jamaica before, haven't you?" Miles asked with a frown.

"Years ago."

"Is that your answer to everything?" Greer demanded in a scornful voice.

"Look at that boat!" Xander cried. I turned my back to Greer to see what Xander was pointing to.

Xander was right. I vaguely remembered my parents bringing my brothers' and I here, and Simon falling into the water. I had no recollection that it was so beautiful—and so much fun.

I had fun with these strangers. Who were now my friends.

At least everyone but Greer. I didn't know what to make of her, and from the way she glared at me every time Miles even smiled at me, I know she didn't like me. But Gillian and Amy and Alicia were great, as were Ari and Xander.

And Miles. He reminded me of my brother Simon so much that it started to hurt being around him. But I didn't let that ache ruin the day.

After we climbed the falls, we ziplined down, shrieking and screaming. Even Xander let out a girlish shout as he skimmed down the water.

After the zip line, we headed back to the catamaran for a rum-punch party.

Gillian found me on the catamaran with cheeks pink from either the sun or the rum. "Having fun?"

I held up my coconut filled with punch. The yellow umbrella tumbled out at the movement. "This is great."

"The rum or the trip?"

"Both."

She turned her back to the party on the deck. "I can't believe Petra gave you her ticket."

"*You* can't! I don't even know her, so I have no idea if it was out character."

Gillian rolled her eyes. "Trust me—it is. But it's good that someone gets to enjoy it, even if she bailed."

We stood at the railing, the breeze whipping my hair into unimaginable knots. While Gillian had been friendly during the day, I had a feeling her seeking me out wasn't purely an overture of friendship. And I didn't have to wait long to find out that I was right.

"Small world that you know Miles," Gillian finally said.

I stifled my groan. "Greer has nothing to worry about."

"It's actually not like her to worry. But I think your history with Miles freaked her out."

"*I* have no history with Miles," I said firmly. "Our families are friends."

"I think it's *your* family history that has her so worried."

"What about my family?" I asked sharply. "What did Miles tell you?"

"Not much, just the basics. Your father's an oil man, mother is a congresswoman, brother is a*dor*able."

"Miles said my brother is adorable?"

"No. I Googled him," Gillian admitted without a hint of remorse.

"I assume you Googled me as well?"

Gillian laughed self-consciously. "Greer did that first thing. There's not much on there about you, by the way."

I closed my eyes with relief. My mother had done her best to keep my story out of the papers but there were always reporters who wouldn't be persuaded with the offer of a sit-down with Congresswoman Park. "I've been off the grid for the last few years."

"Why is that?" She stared expectantly at me, but I only shrugged. "The man problems you mentioned?"

This was beginning to feel like an ambush, friendly or not, and the old Siggy would have told Gillian to mind her own business. "I'm not telling you anything about myself because whatever I say is going straight to Greer. She doesn't like me, so why should I give her any ammunition?"

"It's not that she doesn't like you." I lowered my sunglasses so Gillian saw my raised eyebrow. "It's only that she's getting a bit anxious now that you're in the picture. Especially that I have this." Greer wiggled her fingers and the shiny ring glittered in the sun. "And with Petra and Peter now—I feel sorry for Miles. Greer's upping her game big time."

A peal of laughter followed Gillian's words. When I glanced around, I found Greer, a knockout in a yellow bikini, hanging off Miles' arm as he laughed with Xander.

"She has nothing to worry about from me," I assured her. Especially since Will hadn't been far from my thoughts all day. As much fun as I had with my new friends, I couldn't wait until I got back to the boat to see him.

Later near the end of the excursion, Greer found me at the railing. "You have nothing to worry about from me and Miles," I said as soon as I saw her smug expression.

"Of course not," Greer sneered. "Why would I be worried about you?"

I shrugged. "I have no idea." I turned back to watching the boats in the distance, hoping Greer would take the hint and leave.

But she leaned in beside me. "I've been thinking about Petra a lot today," she said in a sing-song voice. "I've tried to get hold of her, but I can't seem to reach her. I'm really worried."

Fear pricked my stomach. "I told you what happened. She's with Peter."

"That's what *you* say."

"That's what her Instagram said. I checked yesterday and everything was happy hearts and flowers. Lots of emojis."

Greer nodded carefully like she was weighing her words. "I think her uncle might be concerned about how she's not on the boat. Her uncle, the captain."

The catamaran rocked as it hit a wave, causing screams and laughter from the passengers. I watched with dismay as my rum punch-filled coconut fell over the railing, the paper umbrella swaying in the air as it followed.

"Shit," I muttered, watching it sink beneath the waves.

"You lost your drink," Greer said with fake sympathy. "You're going to lose your free cruise too, as soon as I talk to Captain Kellerman."

"Petra said she was going to tell him."

"I'm sure she did, but like you said, she's busy with Peter. And as much as I love her, my bestie isn't that good at remembering things." Greer smiled widely at me as she backed away from the railing. "Hope for your sake she did."

I didn't watch Greer walk away because I didn't want her to see the fear in my eyes.

13

IT WAS A QUIET trip back to the boat. Sunburned and too much rum had made everyone sleepy, so their conversations were short with little laughter. Greer sat with Miles and I felt her gaze on me the entire time. I wondered what she was telling Miles.

Would she really go to the captain? How easy would it be to talk to him? Being the roommate of his niece might give Greer an in, but I couldn't be sure if it was an empty threat or she'd already made plans to carry it out. And what would happen if she did? Would the captain throw me off the ship?

I had an image of me in a life preserver, floating among the waves as the ship leaves me stranded. It was not a pleasant vision.

I wished there was someone I could talk to about the worry that oozed through me.

Deep in thought, I was the last of the group to board the ship but to my surprise, they waited for me.

"So Sigalicious, what are we up to now?" Xander draped an arm around my shoulder. I noticed Greer's frown out of the corner of my eye. Was she really upset that I was friends with Xander? Does she really hate me that much?

"I think I'm heading back to my room for a nap."

"How boring!" Xander cried.

"But sounds like a good idea," Miles said with a laugh. "We can regroup for drinks later before dinner."

"But I'm thirsty now," Xander whined and Miles slapped him on the shoulder.

"There's a good bar on Deck 14 with a really cute bartender," I said but instantly regretted the words. Will had waited for me there yesterday. Would he be there again today? What if he heard this group call me Siggy instead of Petra?

I groaned to myself. I had to tell Will who I was.

"Or there might be one closer to the dining room," I rushed to add.

After a volley of suggestions, it was decided to meet at the wine bar near the dining room. I sighed with relief as Miles turned to me with an expectant smile.

"You'll be there?"

"She'll be having her nap and then going to bed early, won't you, Siggy?" Greer said.

It was the smug smile that did it. If I was going down, it wasn't going to be without a fight.

"I'll be there," I said brightly, baring my teeth with a smile of my own.

I returned to my room to shower off the sunscreen and to take a few minutes to privately freak out.

What would they do to a passenger who had boarded illegally? That would make me a stowaway—I was a stowaway on a cruise ship. What would they do to me?

Why hadn't I thought of this sooner? Why did I ever take Petra's ticket? Some fairy godmother she turned out to be, one with a wicked witch for a best friend.

I didn't have any choice. I had to get off the boat.

Tomorrow we would be in Grand Cayman. I could disembark and then not come back. I would avoid any possible conflict with the captain and make Greer very happy to see the last of me.

Why should I let her win?

I let Charles win when I ran away from home. I ran away from Eduardo because I was afraid to face him and made things worse. Why would I want to do that again?

But staying in Grand Cayman was an option and a good one. I filed it away as I dressed in shorts and a T-shirt, wondering what I should do now—

Will!

We had talked about doing something when I returned from Ocho Rios. How could I have forgotten?

It wasn't until I hurried to Deck 14 that I realized if I was leaving tomorrow, then I would have to say goodbye to Will.

The thought of that sunk heavily in my stomach as I stepped onto the deck.

"Siggy!"

It was Xander, leaning against the bar. He waved me over, and with a quick glance around for Will, I reluctantly joined him. Adonis was nowhere in sight, and I breathed a sigh of relief.

"Why am I not surprised to see you here?"

Xander grinned, his face red from being in the sun all day. "I said I was thirsty. I think I'm dehydrated." He held up his beer glass, with a thick head of foam. "Beer will help."

"I'm sure it will."

"Drink with me," Xander invited.

"I've been drinking with you all day."

"No, you haven't. You've been hiding from my sister." Xander kept his gaze on me as he sipped his beer.

"Your sister doesn't like me," I said carefully.

"My sister doesn't like a lot of people. I'm only here because she likes Miles."

"And that makes me a threat to her because I knew Miles when I was a kid?" I shook my head.

"My sister is under the impression that she needs to get married. Now," Xander explained. "She dragged us on this farce of a romance cruise to make it happen. I mean, the legend of Aphrodite? Have you met your soulmate yet?"

"I don't—I don't think so," I stammered as Xander's eyes lit up.

"You have! Well, I'll be damned! Who?"

"It's no one. It's nothing. He's—nice."

"Nice is good. Is nice cute, too?"

"He's cute." I glanced around. "I think I'm supposed to be meeting him, but I'm not sure where. He was here the last time."

"Sounds even better. Can't wait to meet him."

"You can't." Xander opened his mouth to protest, and I rushed out with an explanation. "He thinks I'm Petra."

"Tell him you're not."

"I can't. What if he gets mad I lied? What if he reports me? I'm basically a stowaway."

Xander cocked his shaggy head. "I guess you kind of are. How did you get on the ship anyway?"

"I used Petra's passport. I lied—I lied to Will because he was the one who checked me in. So he could get in trouble too." I slumped on the stool, my head in my hands. "Plus, if I tell him who I am, he's going to want to know everything about me and there are things I'm not ready to talk about."

"You get more mysterious every day."

"The cruise is going to be over for me because your sister said she's going to tell the captain."

Xander ruefully shook his head. "Of course she's going to tell the captain because that's what Greer does. Sometimes I can't believe she's my sister."

"So you think she will talk to him?" I asked miserably. "I couldn't tell if she was bluffing just as a way to get me to leave Miles alone."

"Oh, Greer's perfectly capable of creating a hornet's nest out of nothing. But don't worry. I won't let her."

"How can you stop her?"

"I won't be able to. But Miles will."

14

I FELT A BIT more optimistic after I talked to Xander, but not entirely out of the water since he gave no indication how Miles would be able to work his magic on Greer to keep her away from the captain.

Xander left me after he finished his beer, assuring me he would find Miles and make sure everything was okay. I had to believe him, even though it was difficult. It had been a while since anyone had looked out for me. And a long time since I had trusted anyone.

It was a scary feeling.

After Xander left, I wandered the deck looking for Will, the butterflies in my stomach becoming more active the more time it took to find him.

I would tell him the truth and everything would be fine.

I would tell him the truth and Will would hate me forever.

I would tell him the truth and Will would not only hate me forever, but he would go straight to the captain, who would throw me off the ship. I would be transported back to Miami, where Eduardo would be waiting for me.

My imagined scenarios got worse and worse.

I rounded the corner on the pool deck, head down against the wind that was doing everything it could be blow me backward.

"Petra—hi!"

Pushing the hair out of my eyes, I saw him. "Will!"

His smile was warm, his brown eyes welcoming. Happiness bloomed in my chest—he looked truly glad to see me.

"I was hoping you'd find me," he said.

"Really?" It would have been so much better if he'd called me by my real name, but I'd take Petra's name one more time. The ship rolled slightly and I took a step sideways to catch my balance.

Will lifted the camera hanging around his neck and I noticed the harried expression on his face. "I have a huge favour. Look, one of our staff photographers is sick and they've asked me to take over."

"Are you a photographer?"

"*No!* And neither is Max, the other cruise director. Both of us assumed it was a smile and click thing, but it's really hard." Will looked faintly embarrassed by the confession. "That's what I was doing all day and I'm ready to chuck this thing overboard. Will you help me? Only for a couple of hours? Walk around and take pictures of people and save the life of this probably very expensive equipment?" He actually put his hands together under his chin and gave me the perfect hangdog expression.

"How can I say no to that?"

"I really hope you can't."

So for the next few hours, I played photographer.

It was a lot of fun, especially since Will never left my side and did most of the talking to the passengers. I soon found out that while he was nice, he was also personable, funny, and had a boatload of charm.

Was that Cupid's arrow digging in deeper?

Why now? Why would I meet a really great guy *now* when I was literally hiding from the world? They said you find your perfect match when you stop looking. I hadn't been looking for years. When I boarded the ship, romance was the last thing on my mind, but now I couldn't seem to get enough of it.

I liked to make him laugh. I liked the way he smiled at me. My skin tingled when he touched me, and I couldn't stand more than two feet away from him without feeling chilled by the warm breeze blowing across the deck.

Will's eyes crinkle in the corners when he smiled. It was a good smile, not as blindingly white as Miles, but sincere. I would guess Will only smiled when he really meant it, unlike Miles who, like me, would have perfected the art of the social smile by the time he was six.

"Have you always been interested in photography?" Will asked as we took a break for water. Taking pictures might have been fun for me, but it was also exhausting, especially after a day outside.

"Since my grandfather gave me one of the first FUJIFILM Instax cameras. My mother was so angry with how much film I used, and how much it cost that she bought me a cheap digital camera." I stared at a family nearby laughing together, one that we had taken pictures of with the blue-and-white life preserver Will lugged around. "My family got so tired of me taking pictures, but never my grandfather. He would sit for hours. I guess he was used to sitting. He's a supreme court judge."

I didn't know why I told him that.

"Really?" Will looked at me with interest. "And what do you do?"

"I'm the stereotypical black sheep," I said breezily, lifting the camera to hide my face. "But I did pretend to work as a fashion photographer to help my brother get a date one time."

"That seems kind of devious."

"Not if you knew my brother. He needed all the help he could get. Simon is great, but a real dork. The girl talked about herself the whole time. We tried something else the next time."

"Like what?"

"Look at that family," I said abruptly. "Let's see if they want their picture taken." I got up, nervous about where the conversation was headed.

I had to tell him the truth, but what would he say?

And then Will smiled at me again, and my good intentions went to pot.

"What are your plans tonight?" Will asked as the pool area began to clear.

"I'm on the late seating for dinner," I said. "And then I think there's talk of the disco later."

"Sounds fun."

"How much of the fun stuff do you get to do?" I asked.

"I get one day and two nights off. Sometimes the day and night are together like this week. I get the day after tomorrow off, and then there's a staff party that night."

"Sounds fun."

"It is. I like what I do. I get to spend time in the sun, meeting interesting people." He poked the camera. "Learning new things."

"You're getting better at taking pictures."

"I've had a good teacher. Feel like helping out again tomorrow if Marty is still under the weather?"

"Sure, but..."

"You don't have to."

"I want to," I said honestly, looking forward to spending more time together. But Greer if goes to the captain—I push the thoughts of Greer out of my mind. "If you want me to."

"I kind of *need* you," Will admitted with a sheepish grin. "But it's a good way to get to hang out together. I *want* to do that."

"Me too." We stared at each other, the air charged with electricity like before a storm. It would be the perfect time for a kiss.

"I'm really glad I met you, Petra."

Cold water splashed against the backs of my legs as a kid cannonballed into the pool. I moved away, the moment broken by Petra's name rather than the splash.

I needed to tell him the truth. I opened my mouth. "So what do you do on your day off?"

I was such a coward. I always have been. I had run away from my problems, I hid when things got difficult. Why should today with Will be any different?

I stopped the self-abasement in time to focus on what Will was saying.

"It'll be in Cozumel, so I'm going ashore. There's this great place in the jungle that I like to go to." He paused and looked at me closely. "Do you have plans for Cozumel?"

I honestly had no idea if I did or not. Or whether I would still be on the boat.

"I think I'm playing it by ear."

"Did you want to go with me?"

I paused, full of excuses. But something about Will—his smile or the blue of his eyes—stopped me from giving him a fast and firm no.

"I'd love to."

15

Day Four - Grand Cayman, Cayman Islands

WHEN WE REACHED GRAND Cayman the next day, I was one of the last passengers off the boat. I heard the excited talk about turtles and Stingray City last night at dinner, but hadn't taken part.

Dinner was much better last night because Greer wasn't there. But even with her absence, I said good night to the group after we finished eating, and headed back to my room.

I had a lot to think about.

Georgetown, Grand Cayman was like a second home to me. My parents owned a condo on Seven Mile Beach and I had spent countless school holidays there. I knew practically every inch of the island. I'd fed the turtles at Cayman Turtle Farm, and I'd swum with the stingrays. I'd explored the wrecks. I'd been to Hell.

I didn't need an excursion. I could lead a tour for one.

As I disembarked, I bumped into a chattering group of passengers. The short woman in the middle had her camera up to film to the view of Georgetown.

"Holly, finish up," ordered a tall, dark-haired man. "I don't want to be late."

"If you go into the middle of town, you can get a great picture of the cruise ships docked," I suggested as I walked by, my own camera out and ready.

Tall and Dark caught my gaze. "Coming from the Aphrodite?"

When I nodded, the woman stopped filming and turned to me. "Would you mind taking our picture?" she asked with a smile, holding out her camera.

"Sure." I waited until they posed, touching, but not enough to suggest they were a couple. "Do you want your friend in it too?" A man hovered behind me, not much older than Tall and Dark with the misfortune to wear sandals with a pair of black socks pulled up to mid-calf.

He reminded me of my father, who hated bare feet.

"We're off to Stingray City," the woman said after I handed the camera back.

"It's pretty amazing," I assured her. "I'm off to the beach. Have a great time!" With a quick wave, I sidestepped them, leaving the woman chattering to the man about the stingrays.

The walk from the pier to Seven Mile Beach was easy but filled with memories of my family. My brothers were everywhere. My mother was right beside me, holding my hand as we skipped through the waves. And my father—

The disappointment in his face still haunted me. The unasked questions—how could I have let such a man into our family? How could I be so stupid? It was the image of my father's expression that held me back when the homesickness got too much, the memory of his anger that stopped me from calling home.

Those memories had faded into a dull black and white by the time I got to the row of condos on the beach.

I watched for a few minutes to make sure the condo was empty. Residents and renters filled the balconies overlooking the water and lounge chairs dotted the sand. It was April; no school breaks so there were no children in the water.

This was a good thing since kids were much more observant when it came to noticing something out of the ordinary.

My parents' condo was on the second level. It was a double unit, with lots of room for family or my mother to gift it to potential campaign donators for a weekend. I never took much notice of the security system whenever I was there, but a quick glance through the window suggested it would be easy to bypass if for some reason the password had changed.

My little lock-picking kit made quick work of the door, and the password was the same as it had always been. Once inside I took a deep breath. The air in the condo was stale from being shut up for a few weeks, but if I concentrated I could smell the hint of garlic. My father loved garlic, especially when he grilled steaks, cooking them to a tender rare, with a tinge of blood left on the plate.

The phone was on the desk. I dialled the number from memory, without giving myself a moment to change my mind.

"Congresswoman Park's office."

"Stella...hi. It's Siggy. Seraphina. How are you?"

My mother's assistant gave a sharp intake of breath. "Siggy! Siggy? How are you—where are you? Your mother—"

"Is she there?"

"She's in a briefing but—hang on. Wait one minute and I'll tell her it's you. Oh, Siggy, it's so good to hear from you!"

Stella was gone before I had a chance to respond. The next minute was the longest of my life but then my mother was on the line.

"Seraphina? Are you okay?"

"Hi, Mom."

"Oh, Siggy."

My knees gave out and I crumpled to the floor. My mother—the tough-as-nails congresswoman famous for her stance on drugs and abortion and funding for Planned Parenthood—was crying. That was all I needed for my own waterworks to start.

"I'm okay," I said quickly, wiping my nose as a tear leaked out of my eyes. "I'm fine. I miss you."

As I walked along the beach, I had rehearsed what I was going to say but it flew out of my head as soon as I heard my mother's voice.

"Siggy...I miss you too."

"I'm sorry. I'm so sorry about Charles."

"Oh, sweetheart, there's nothing for you to be sorry about. He fooled all of us. You couldn't have known what he was like."

"But it's my fault—"

"Siggy, please stop. Now tell me where you are and I'll send the car."

"Well, that might be a little difficult." When I told her I was in Grand Cayman, she didn't bat an eyelash even when I told her I'd broken into the condo. I explained about the cruise, skirting the details of Petra's passport. I left out everything about my life in Miami, just telling her it was where I'd been hiding out.

"I want you to come home," she said, her voice firm and unyielding. "I can get a plane to you by tomorrow. You can stay at the condo until then."

"No, I'll get back on the boat." This surprised me as much as it did her. "I'll fly home from Miami on Saturday."

"I want you here now." Her voice changed to wistful and sad, which was more effective than the tough voice, but I held firm.

I wasn't ready to leave Will, but it wasn't just him. I didn't want to run away again. Even if Greer and the captain met me on deck, I was returning to the boat.

"It's only a few days," I reassured her, laughing through my tears. "I'll be home soon."

"About Charles," she said. "There are things you need to know."

"I don't want to know anything about him."

"He was arrested six months ago. He's in jail, Siggy. He can't do anything to hurt you ever again."

"Jail! What happened?"

She chuckled. "He got greedy, tried the same scam again, only this time it didn't go as planned. You were the fourth wife he had, Siggy. But not for long, because I have the divorce papers at home, waiting for your signature. You can put all this behind you."

But I couldn't. And I wouldn't ever forget.

16

I STAYED AT THE condo for the afternoon, eating stale crackers and watching the waves roll into the shore until it was time to head back to the boat.

I was excited to see Will. It was time to tell him everything.

Back on board, after a quick trip to my cabin to drop off my bag, I took my camera and rushed to meet Will by the pool as planned.

"Petra!"

I vowed that would be the last time Will would call me by another woman's name.

"How was Cayman?"

"It was...enlightening," I said with a smile, recalling the conversation with my mother.

Will frowned. "I don't normally hear Cayman called enlightening. Turtles or stingrays?"

I shook my head. "Neither. A walk along the beach."

"You had a nice day for it. Not too hot, not too busy."

"It was perfect."

We stood, the noise of the pool fading around us. It was time, the perfect time. "Will, I—"

"Ready to take some pictures?" Will asked at the same time. "As long as you don't have other plans, of course. I talked to Marty and she's still not feeling great. She was able to work for most of the day, but I told her I'd do a couple of hours for her. If you'd help."

I melted at the sight of his smile. "Sure." Then, "Marty is a girl. Woman?"

Will nodded, his head bobbing like a bobblehead. "I told her all about you. Well, the little I know, anyway. She's really grateful for you helping out. She can't wait to see your pictures."

Marty was a girl. A girl *friend* or a sharing-the-bunk girl-friend?

Suddenly it didn't seem that important to tell Will my real name.

"Hey, I know you!" A hand tugged on mine. I pulled my attention away from Will to see a blond boy with a wide smile staring expectantly at me. "You're the girl when we got on the boat."

I recognized him as Sam, the ferret-loving little boy I'd met as I boarded the ship. "I am. And you're Sam."

"You remember my name?"

"I remember everyone who has a ferret. How's Mr. Feeney?" I asked Sam and gave him a wink before raising my camera. "Say cheese!"

We spent a while taking pictures of the family. When even Sam seemed tired of the poses, I finished up with a great action shot of Sam's little sister jumping into the water and thanked the family for their time. As Will handed the father the card detailing when and where to view the pictures, Sam tugged on my arm again. "I've got something else you can take a picture of."

"What's that?"

"It's in my cabin. C'mon."

"Wait, you've got to tell your parents."

But Sam didn't want his parents to come with him, so after a few minutes of heated conversation, they allowed Will and I to follow Sam to his cabin, which was only a deck down.

"They let their kid walk around with strangers?" Will whispered as we hurried to catch up with Sam. For a kid with short legs, he was pretty quick.

"Maybe they want to get rid of him for a couple of minutes. Great kid, but lots of energy. Plus, you're in a uniform, so you're official."

He gestured to my shorts and tank top. "You're not."

"Yes, but they think I'm nice. Also, I'm very cute. I'm not threatening."

"You are very cute."

I glanced quickly at Will, who was smiling at me. Warmth pooled in my stomach and I couldn't stop the grin from spreading across my face. "It's nice of you to notice."

"I'm very nice too."

"And cute?"

Another moment, another smile between us was interrupted. "Here's my room!" Sam cried, waving the key card his mother had pressed into his hand and cautioned not to lose. With a swipe, he opened the door and tumbled into the room.

As soon as the door opened, something brown darted out, running down the hall toward us like a flat and furry bowling ball.

A scream cut the air and I was pretty sure it wasn't from me.

"Mr. Feeney!"

Instinct, and years of growing up with hamsters and guinea pigs prompted me to drop to my knees, hands at the ready like I was about to catch a baseball.

Of course I missed the ferret, and a second scream cut the air as the little body scampered over Will's foot.

"Mr. Feeny, wait!" Sam shouted.

"I don't think he's listening," I muttered, swiveling to make a grab for the quick as lightning creature. My fingers felt the coarse hair, but the animal moved quicker than I did.

"What is that thing?" gasped Will.

"He's a ferret," Sam said with disgust. He darted into the room to get a bag of ferret food. "Mr. Feeney—treat!"

Amazingly, the little critter stopped and stood up on his short back legs, whiskers twitching as it sniffed the air in the direction of the treat.

"Good boy." I reached out and scooped him up, giving him back to Sam, who cuddled him under his chin.

"You shouldn't have that thing on board," Will said in a shaky voice.

"He's not a thing; he's Mr. Feeney. And you scream like a girl."

"You kind of do." I laughed.

Apparently, Sam's parents had no idea Sam had smuggled his pet on board, despite this being the third escape attempt by Mr. Feeney. They were aghast when Will told them. I felt bad for Sam who stood with head bowed contritely.

"Are you going to throw him overboard?" Sam asked in a wavering voice. He turned to me with big blue eyes filled with tears and my heart clutched in my chest.

"No, the captain frowns on throwing anything overboard," Will said sternly.

"Are you going to tell the captain?" Sam wailed.

"If you promise to keep him contained in your room, I don't see any need to mention this to anyone else." Will frowned in Sam's direction but when the little boy lifted his gaze, Will winked at him.

"I'll find a better box," Sam promised as we waved goodbye to the family.

"Maybe one of those rat traps," Will muttered as we waved goodbye to the family.

"You really don't like ferrets?"

Will shook his head. "Anything furry. Last year, my buddy Lincoln organized a Pets Onboard cruise and everyone brought their pets." He shuddered. "It was a disaster."

"You're not a pet person, like dogs and cats pets?"

"I can handle them from a distance. But it's rodent-like things that really get me. Rats, squirrels...skunks."

"Everyone should be afraid of skunks."

He hunched his shoulders. "I was sprayed by a skunk when I was a kid. We were at a friends' cottage, and I had to—you know—in the middle of the night."

"Pee?" I guessed.

"I was seven. It was a long walk to the outhouse, so I just stood by the backdoor and peed off the porch. I never even saw the skunk, and well, kind of got him."

I burst out laughing. "I bet you smelled him, though."

"Yeah." Will rubbed the back of his neck. "He got me back pretty good. No one would play with me for the rest of the weekend. I spent a lot of time in the water. By myself."

After another hour, Will took the memory card out of the camera. "You're tired," he said. "You're on a cruise. I can't monopolize you for the whole time. You need some time to relax."

Will's look suggested he wanted to monopolize my whole time. Another pool of warmth began in my stomach, but this time it mixed with a sour taste in my stomach. I still haven't told him my real name. I reluctantly handed him the camera.

"I'll take this to Marty. You have a good night. We're still on for tomorrow?"

I nodded. I would tell him tomorrow.

17

AFTER WILL LEFT ME, I headed back to my cabin to change for dinner. I was tempted to take a quick nap but instead I took the iPad out to the balcony and looked up Charles.

My mother was right—it was all there, spread all over the internet for anyone to see. Fortunately, neither my family nor I were mentioned. Instead, they talked about Carolina Kirsch, a wealthy socialite from New York who discovered what Charles had been trying to do before it was too late.

Looks like Charles bit off more than he could chew with his new bride.

I watched as the waves kicked and rolled behind the boat, as the coast of Grand Cayman grew smaller. Tomorrow we would be in Cozumel, Mexico, and the next day we'd be headed back to Miami.

By Saturday, we would be back on American soil.

Excitement buzzed under my skin as I dressed for dinner. Maybe it was the knowledge I would have my family at my side when I dealt with Eduardo; maybe just knowing they were behind me brought about new confidence. As I dressed for dinner, I felt good.

How much did Will had to do with that?

I put on another one of Petra's dresses and headed up to Deck 14 for my usual stop at Parnassus bar.

"My lady." Adonis was once again behind the glossy bar and nodded his godlike head at me. "What can I get you? Nectar of the gods?"

"Is that what we're calling a martini tonight?"

"Coming right up."

I stood at the bar, turned sideways to watch the action flowing by. It was easy to pick out the passengers who had come from the early seating for dinner because they had pink cheeks and smiles on their faces, and many walked slower because of too much food.

I smiled as an older couple strolled by, the man clutching his stomach with a satisfied expression on his face. As I watch, the woman slipped her arm through his.

It wasn't only the younger generation who were looking for love. I watched the couple, wondering if they had met on board, or if they were there celebrating a milestone in their life.

"Your drink, my lady."

I turned to thank Adonis and saw Will in the mirror behind the bar.

He was leading a small group of sunburned passengers to Hestia restaurant beside Parnassus. His eyes widened as he caught sight of me and a smile brightened his face.

I waved before he disappeared from sight.

A moment later he reappeared and came straight to my side. "Hey. Fancy seeing you here," Will said after he saw his group to their table at the pizza place.

"Are you playing maître d' now?"

"My work is never done." Will nodded at Adonis and leaned closer. "You look absolutely amazing."

I looked in the mirror before I left the room. I knew I looked good. Petra's dress—a gauzy maxi dress was loose and comfortable, and the purple was a perfect colour for me. I couldn't be bothered to straighten my hair, so my curls were wild.

"Thanks," I said with a smile.

"How come you're all alone? And no camera?"

"No one likes it when I take pictures with their mouths full."

"Thanks again for your help today. And yesterday. I think, with your help, I might be able to take a picture without cutting off heads."

"Sometimes the headless shots are the best ones." I sipped my martini and Will nodded his approval.

"Pre-dinner drink. Adonis does make a good martini."

"Is that from experience?" Something had changed between us. It felt like it was a lifetime ago that he followed me around as I took pictures of the passengers, posing them against the railing, before the smokestack, with the waves behind them.

I wish it was Will I was meeting for dinner.

"I do get the occasional night off. Like tonight, for instance," he said lightly. Then his face fell. "Sort of. My buddy works at the disco and there's a big dance-off thing tonight that I promised to help with. You should come!"

He sounded as excited as Sam was earlier.

"To a dance off? Do I have to dance?"

"Do you like to dance?"

An image of my pole-dance lesson flashed in my mind. "I love to dance, but I'm not sure if I'm ready to *off* something with my moves."

He laughed. "It'd be fun to watch."

"I'll see what I can do. It's been a long day so I might have an early night." As soon as I heard my words, I winced. "I sound like an old lady, don't I? Oh, young man, I'm too tired to go out tonight," I said in a creaky, old-lady voice.

"I think you've got a while to go before we put you in a home."

"I like to sleep," I confessed. "Naps are my favourite. I can fall asleep anywhere."

"Anywhere?"

"I once fell asleep on a toilet in a bar. And I wasn't that drunk."

With a laugh, Will backed away. "I'd better go. I want to hear what happened on the toilet tomorrow," he said.

"You really don't," I assured him. "I'll come up with something better to entertain you with."

Like stories about what I'd been doing for the past four years.

Mickey the maitre d' greeted me with a smile when I arrived at Mount Olympus. "A glass of champagne tonight, miss?"

"I think I'm good," I said. Even with a showdown with Greer looming over my head, I was still full of Will's smile.

There were a few empty seats when I was shown to the table. "Greer not joining us?" I asked lightly as I took the seat beside Xander.

"Apparently she's still not feeling well," Xander said. If it wasn't for the twinkle in his eyes, he could have passed for a concerned older brother. "And Miles is passed out in our cabin, so you, my sweet Sigalicious—" He threw a heavy arm around my shoulder. "—are my drinking partner for the evening."

"Better you than me." Ari raised his glass to me. Alicia was seated on the other side of Ari and when I smiled a greeting at her, I noticed a new face.

"This is Sayid," Alicia said, her cheeks pink. "We met at the waterfall."

I vaguely remembered seeing Alicia with the tall, dark and handsome stranger. I might not have known Alicia well, but I knew the signs of a woman in love. And Alicia had all of them.

It looked like Cupid's arrow had struck again.

18

Day 5 - Cozumel, Mexico

T HE NEXT MORNING AT seven o'clock on the dot, there was a knock on the door. "Why does he have to be the punctual type?" I muttered as I threw my sunscreen and an extra T-shirt in my bag before I opened the door.

Petra's bag. Petra's T-shirt.

"Morning, Petra."

It was easy enough to forget I was playing a part when I was by myself, or even with Miles and his friends, but it was becoming increasingly difficult to do so with Will.

"Hi, Will." He stepped inside the room, even though there was no invite. It wasn't that I didn't want him there, but it was a little embarrassing to have him see it like this. Clothes were strewn all over the place, thrown about in my attempt to find something in Petra's wardrobe that looked even remotely like something I'd buy for myself.

I made do with my cutoffs and a purple tank top I unearthed that still had the price tag on it.

"This is *your* room?" Will asked, wandering farther in. "I mean, I know it's your room, but just you? It's so big to be staying in by yourself."

"I had a friend who was supposed to come with me," I lied. "When she bailed, I kept the room because it looked...pretty."

He turned to me. "It is very pretty."

My stomach had never done an actual somersault before.

"Thanks. It's a bit of a mess right now." Were we still talking about the room?

"Does it matter? You're on vacation."

"But you're not." I pushed him towards the door and grabbed my bag. "Since you made me get up so early, let's go make the most of your day off."

Will had already gotten our disembarking tickets and with him by my side, it was a breeze to get off the boat. We were driving away from Cozumel in no time.

"Do you go to this mysterious place every time you're in port?" I leaned back against the back seat of the taxi, knowing that I was going to end up with sweat marks on the back of my shirt.

"Does it bug you that I haven't told you where we're going?" Will's grin was both infuriating and infectious; his dimples were out in full force and his eyes crinkled in the most adorable way.

He was so cute.

"It's driving me crazy!" I cried with mock frustration. "I love surprises, but I hate being surprised."

"That doesn't make sense."

"It does," I insisted. "Surprises are fun but it's the anticipation of knowing you'll be surprised that drives me crazy."

"Would you have rather me kidnap you at breakfast and throw you in the back of the car so you have no idea of what's going on?"

"That actually sounds like a story from *60 Minutes*!"

"I guess. Just so you know, I've never kidnapped anyone."

"I'm really glad to hear that."

"I thought it was a good selling feature."

I laughed, thinking again how cute he was. "I still don't like being surprised."

"Poor Petra."

And that made him less cute. Or maybe made *me* less cute. I turned to the window. The cityscape of Cozumel was gone, already transformed into the jungle.

I had to tell him that I wasn't Petra, and that I was a stowaway on his cruise ship.

Will leaned over and pointed to a road we were approaching. "Sometimes I stop at this village down there. The kids are adorable. I try to bring them little things because they don't have a lot."

His cuteness level was back and just flew off the chart.

We chatted as the taxi driver took us farther into the jungle. Will told me about his sisters, and I responded with true stories about my brothers.

It was one of the first things Eduardo taught me, that it was easy to be believable when you told at least part of the truth. But in this case, I wanted to be honest with Will. I wanted him to know me. I wanted to tell him about talking to my mother yesterday, and how it made me feel.

But I couldn't. Not now. Not when I had no idea where I was, or where I was going. Because what if he didn't like what I told him? Or didn't like me?

"We're almost there," Will said shortly.

"Still not telling me anything?"

"I think you'll have fun. I know *I'll* have fun with you."

Twenty minutes later, I was being lowered via harness into a hole in the earth. "It's fine, Petra," Will repeated, over and over again.

"I don't think it is." I clutched the rope with both hands as I was swung lower and lower into the hole. A dank smell rose up. Wet dirt and moss and something I couldn't identify and didn't want to think about. "I don't think—what is this?"

It was a cave, a cavern. A *cenote*. A big black hole in the earth filled with water.

"It's so cool!"

"Unhook and drop into the water," Will called from far above. "Grab one of the inner tubes and I'll be right down."

A few minutes later, Will was beside me in the water. I had pulled one of the black inflatable donuts over my head, and rested my arms on the side as my legs dangled in the cool water. The *cenote* was lit only by the sunlight peering through into the hole at the top, and so dark at the water I couldn't see the sides of the cave.

Of course, Will tugged my tube into the darkness.

It was peaceful, once I got past being terrified that a dianoga was going to pull me out of my tube and under the water. I told Will as much.

"You said dianoga." Will stared at me with something akin to awe. "Which means you know what it is."

"The thing that pulls Luke under when they're stuck in the trash compactor," I said disdainfully. The scene was classic for any *Star Wars* fan.

"Did you have a boyfriend that forced you to watch the *Star Wars* movies?" Will asked hesitantly.

"Brothers. But now I watch them for me."

"You're into Star Wars," Will mused aloud, staring up into the darkness. "You let me drop you into a hole in the ground without freaking. You might be the perfect woman."

"You'd better believe it."

Suddenly Will disappeared into the black water. "Will?" I called nervously. His head popped up beside my tube, making me lose my grip. "Don't do that!"

"Do what?"

"Scare me like that."

He smiled as he hooked his arms on my tube and pulled me closer. "Maybe you're not the perfect woman if you don't like to be scared. Or surprised."

"We were just talking about Luke getting pulled under and then you disappear? See how you like it!" Holding my breath, I slid out of the tube, disappearing under the water and resurfacing beside Will.

He laughed. "That doesn't count because I was expecting it."

"Are you expecting this?" With one hand on my tube, I pulled him to me with the other, leaning up to press my lips against his.

Will's lips were soft and gentle and wet. As he deepened the kiss, my hand left the tube and wound around his neck, which promptly sank us both.

I came up laughing, with Will's hands around my waist. "Maybe get back into the tube," Will suggested with a chuckle. "I don't want to lose you in the water." He lowered the donut over my head and I rested my arms on the side.

Then he kissed me again. And again. And again, as we drifted in the cool, dark water. Will kissed me until they told us our time was up and we were pulled out of the *cenote*. And then he kissed me in the taxi all the way back to Cozumel, which made me miss all the scenery.

Not that I was complaining.

Once we were back in the city, I showed Will just how perfect I was when we stopped at Will's favourite restaurant for lunch. Not only did I dare him to eat one of the jalapenos in my spicy margarita, but I also popped one in my mouth as well.

"You like spicy foods." He grinned, even as he grabbed for his glass of water.

"I like all food," I confessed. "I'm part Hispanic and part Korean, so I grew up with every kind of heat. My father used to hide the bottles of hot sauce in the kitchen because my mother hated the stuff. But since she practically never went into the kitchen, it was okay."

"She doesn't cook?"

"Unless it's for a big holiday. She usually helps out for Thanksgiving, but cooking is my dad's thing. And Carmelia." Just saying her name brought on a wave of homesickness. Carmelia had been with our family since my little brother had been born when I was five.

All of a sudden I couldn't believe how much I missed her cooking. I missed her smile. And her hugs...

"Who's Carmelia?"

"Our housekeeper." My voice thickened with emotion. "But she's really more than that. My parents worked so much when I was growing up that Carmelia practically raised me and my brothers."

"What do your parents do that made them so busy?"

This was getting into true confessions. But since I wanted Will to know who I was—"My mother is a congresswoman, my dad is president of an oil company."

It was hard not to be impressed with parents like mine and Will didn't even try to hide it. Talking about them made me miss my family even more. If I hadn't spoken to my mother yesterday, I didn't think I could have borne it.

But knowing that I'd be home in a few days made it easier. Home, with my parents and my brothers.

Will smiled at me through a mouthful of burrito.

After lunch, we walked through town, stopping at little shops so I could buy my fill of souvenirs. We ended up at a nearby beach, waiting for the last minute to board the ship. The day passed me by in a happy haze of Will, his smile, his laughter, his dizzying kisses.

I didn't remember the last time I'd been so happy. I pushed aside any thoughts of the cruise ending, of not sharing another day like this with Will and focused on the here and the now. Excuse followed excuse as the sun sank into the sky. I knew I couldn't wait much longer. He needed to know the truth.

And I needed to stop wincing every time Will called me another woman's name because he was going to catch me before long.

"So tell me about having a congresswoman for a mother," Will said as we waded barefoot in the water, holding hands. "My mom was head of the PTA, so I can see the similarities."

"It was her job. She went to work, sometimes came home really late. Sometimes she had to stay in Washington. One of the strangest things was my teacher asking her if my class could visit the State Department. We did, and there was Mom, in her suit, being all congresswoman-y. It was kind of surreal. And now, she's on Twitter, so I get all these tweets from her that thousands of people like—or not like. She has trolls, which is difficult." I couldn't look at Will. "I haven't seen her in almost four years."

Will looked confused. "Why not? From the way you talk about your family, I'd say you were close."

I took a deep breath. "I left home. Ran away from home, actually."

He smiled. "You're how old, Petra? I don't think you can call it running away from home."

"My name isn't Petra."

It was more of a mic stand crashing through the floor than a simple drop and Will dropped my hand like it was made of ice. "What is your name then?"

"Siggy. Well, Seraphina Park-Smith, but everyone calls me Siggy."

"Why are you calling yourself Petra?" He sounded confused but I heard the touch of anger.

I took another breath, this one so deep it made me dizzy. "Here's where things get complicated."

"How complicated?"

"Kind of a lot, so please listen because I don't know if I can finish if I don't get it done in one fell swoop. I'm married."

"Married." Even with his carefully composed expression, I saw the anger in his eyes.

"I only found out he's in jail, and the divorce papers are waiting for me to sign, so I won't be married for long. He's a bad man." I held up a hand as Will opened his mouth. "I really like how you ask questions, but hold on a minute. Charles married me to get his hands on my trust fund, and my parents' money. As you can imagine, there's a lot of money in my family. Charles used me, stole almost a million dollars and threatened to destroy my mother's career if we didn't give him more.

"I couldn't let that happen, so I ran away. If he couldn't find me, he couldn't hurt my parents."

"And that's why you haven't seen them?" Will asked carefully.

I nodded. "But yesterday, I broke into their condo in Grand Cayman and—"

"Wait a minute, you *broke* in?"

"For the past year, I'd been running cons, with a bit of small-time B & E on the side," I confessed. "Small stuff. I never hurt anyone. But yes, I'm pretty good at breaking into places."

"You're a criminal?"

"No. Maybe. I guess you could call me that." There was no reply from Will, so I rushed forward. "Not a bad one. And not a very good one. I messed up my first job and owe

Eduardo money... I'm not excusing what I've done, but when I left home, I got caught up with some people. I was angry at Charles, and I wanted to use people like he used me. It wasn't a good thing to do, it wasn't smart, but that's why. And it's kind of the short version of why Petra isn't my real name," I finished, realizing that my explanation wasn't a very good one.

"Who's the real Petra?"

My heart cracked at the cold steel of his voice.

"That's where it gets a little more complicated. She, uh, gave me the tickets for the cruise. She thought I was an Uber driver and I was taking her to the boat when she got a call from the guy she was in love with, and then she gave me the tickets and her suitcase because the guy proposed," I said in a rush.

Will shook his head. "You can't get on board without a passport, and the passport has to match the name on the ticket. *I* checked your passport!"

"That was Petra's."

"You used someone's passport to board. That's illegal," he said flatly.

My heart sank. "I know that. But I needed to get away from Miami and Petra—Petra really wanted me to go."

Will stood up. I wanted to reach for his hand, but the stiffness of his body told me not to. "We should get back to the boat."

"Will..."

"What am I supposed to call you?"

"Siggy," I said in a low voice.

"I kissed you, and I didn't even know your real name." He shook his head. "I could get fired for this, you know. You're some spoiled little rich girl playing at being bad and you don't care at all about what happens to me."

"No, Will, that's not it I do care—"

Will turned his back and started to walk away.

"Will, wait! Please—"

He stopped and spoke without turning around. "How am I supposed to believe you when you've been lying to me the entire time? I think you can get back to the boat yourself."

And then he kept walking.

19

I WAITED A SUITABLE time, sitting at the beach and trying to keep the tears from flooding my eyes before heading back to the boat. I didn't want to trail behind Will, waiting impatiently for any crumb he might deign to throw back at me.

I shouldn't have worried because he was long gone when I boarded. There was no sign of his wavy dark hair or the smile that I'd looked forward to seeing more than anything else on the ship.

I lied to Will and it hurt so much that I'd upset him so badly. And what he said about me, about me being a spoiled rich girl just playing and not caring? Was that the truth?

Before heading to my cabin to spend what was going to be a very long and painful evening, I stopped for supplies, a strawberry daiquiri and a huge ice cream cone. The daiquiri was already gone when I bumped into Miles.

"Siggy, hey! Missed you in Cozumel today."

"I had plans with a friend." I was glad I still wore my sunglasses so Miles wouldn't see my reddened eyes.

"Good plans?" He raised an eyebrow. "Good friend? Xander told me you met someone."

I shrugged, taking a miserable lick from my cone. It was beginning to melt in the heat, already dripping down my hand.

"You okay?" For a minute Miles sounded exactly like my brother Simon and I was tempted to dump my troubles on his sympathetic shoulder.

"I'm fine."

"Uh uh." Miles turned me in place and marched me to the elevator. "I know what it means when a woman says she's fine. Let's go, back to your cabin. You're going to need to clean yourself up if you don't eat that quickly."

"Ice cream sounded like a good idea," I said, licking at the melting chocolate.

After Miles insisted on a tour of the cabin, we settled on the balcony. I finished my ice cream and washed the chocolate off my hands before pulling out two bottles of beer from the fridge.

"I can't believe Petra got this place all to herself! Greer was so annoyed because they were supposed to share a room, and then Petra booked a single. Greer is rooming with Amy and Alicia because there wasn't another single left open and she's not happy about it."

"Being here with you all makes me feel like I kind of know Petra."

"Well, she's kind of exactly like Greer," Miles admitted. "Sometimes I can't believe they're friends. They're always vying for attention."

"How is Greer?" I asked, wanting to inquire if Miles had been able to work any magic on her before she visited the captain. But suddenly it didn't matter if I was to be thrown off, as long as Will didn't get into trouble for allowing me on.

"I'm not here to talk about Greer," Miles said in a firm voice. "What's going on with you and that long face? It's not Siggylike."

"You haven't seen me in years. How would you know what Siggy is like?"

Miles leaned back in his chair with an affectionate smile on his handsome face. "Do you remember the party your parents had for Christmas one year? I think you were seventeen. Simon had just turned twenty-one—"

"And the two of you got me drunk," I finished with a rueful laugh.

"I seem to recall you getting yourself drunk."

"How can you recall what happened when you had more to drink than I did?"

"I'd been drinking legally for six months by then and that was the first time you'd had a drink."

"Oh, it was, was it?"

Miles looked wounded. "It wasn't? I always liked thinking I was your first time."

His words hung between us. "I had such a crush on you back then." I sighed, remembering eighteen-year-old me and how a smile from Miles could make my day.

"I know," Miles surprised me by saying.

I narrowed my eyes at him. "How could you know?"

"Your brother told me?"

"Simon?" I cried. "That jerk! How did he—?"

"It was Sam," Miles admitted. "I think he might have read your diary."

"That little...I'll—" I didn't finish my threat as Miles laughed.

"They must miss you."

"I talked to my mother yesterday," I said quietly. "I'm going home after we get to Miami."

"I'm really glad, Siggy." Sincerity rang in Miles' voice. "I don't understand why you left, but I'm sure you had your reasons."

I squinted into the brightness of the sky. "It really doesn't seem like that good of a reason now."

We watched the waves; Miles finished his beer and got another one. "Are you going to tell me what's wrong?" he asked as he sat back down.

"It's nothing...Actually, that's not true. It's big deal to someone." I took a deep breath, thinking about the hurt on Will's face. "I lied about who I was."

"Who is this someone? Does it matter what he thinks of you?"

I nodded. "It matters a lot. After Saturday, I'll never see him again and I have to leave knowing that he hates me."

"No one can hate you, Siggy."

"Will has every reason to. For the whole cruise, he's been thinking I was Petra because I used her passport to get on board."

Miles burst out laughing. "That's why he's mad? Sorry," he said, fixing his face into a more solemn expression. "That's why he's mad at you. Why didn't you tell him your real name? There aren't many people who would want to be Petra, at least not the people who know her."

"Because I was afraid I'd get kicked off the boat. Last time I heard, pretending to be someone else was frowned on. Illegal, even."

"You've got a point there."

"And since I haven't exactly been an outstanding citizen lately, I didn't want any attention."

"What have you been into?"

I waved the beer bottle at him. "That's a story for another time, one with a lot more beer."

"I'll hold you to that. Have you told your friend—"

"Will," I supplied.

"Your friend, Will, why you lied?"

"He really didn't give me a chance."

"Did you ask for a chance or did you run and hide?"

"I'm not sure." I thought back. I hadn't run, but I certainly hadn't pressed the issue, either. I'd just let Will walk away from me.

"Maybe you can find him and talk to him. That's what I'd do."

"What if he doesn't want to talk to me? What if he thinks I'm a horrible person?"

"Then you have to convince him otherwise. You've got a day left to do it."

"A day," I said, my brain whirling with what I could do, how I could make Will forgive me. "Thanks, Miles."

"You're very welcome."

We sat quietly, both lost in our thoughts for long minutes.

"So what's going on with you and Greer?" I asked finally.

"Absolutely nothing."

"That's too bad. Gillian said she really likes you."

"Greer is...oblivious." Miles sighed. "She just sees what she wants to see. She knows full well I have no interest in her, yet she continues to chase after me."

"Have you *told* her you're not interested?" I asked tactfully, thinking Miles' continual presence would make it difficult for a smitten woman to take a hint.

He looked at me like I had two heads. "I'm in love with Xander, Siggy."

The legs of my deck chair came crashing down. "You're what?"

"You didn't know?"

I thought back on what I knew of Xander and Miles, what I'd seen of their interactions. Friendly, but not overly romantic. But wait—

"You were always sitting together at dinner, and on the bus. Guy friends don't usually do that when there's a girl to sit with."

"I thought Greer might get the hint," Miles said miserably.

"And all this time she's been hating on me because she thinks I'm trying to steal you" I threw up my hands. "And here you are, in love with her brother! Now she can hate Xander. Although, really, who can hate Xander?"

"I certainly don't."

"So he feels the same way?"

Miles smiled sheepishly. "So he says."

I turned to Miles with a huge grin. "I'm so happy for you. This is great news."

"I'm glad you think it's great," he grumbled. "Because when I get home and tell my mother that you were on the cruise with me, the first thing she's going to do is try and set us up. I haven't told them about Xander yet—about any of this."

"Ah."

Miles finished his beer. "My problems are going to take a lot more beer than this to fix. Your mess, on the other hand, we can fix."

I stared at my bare toes resting on the balcony railing.

"Find him, Siggy, and tell him how you feel. You'll always regret it if you don't."

I missed half of the dinner by scouring the ship for Will. I stopped at ducking into the staff quarters because passengers weren't allowed, but ran through every deck looking for him, asking every staff member I came across, but no one had seen him.

Eventually, I headed to Mount Olympus dining room, convinced Will was still in Cozumel.

Miles was seated beside Xander, both with big smiles on their faces. Both of them rested a hand on the table, barely touching. I looked around with dismay to find there was no empty seat waiting for me.

"We didn't think you were coming, Siggy," Alicia apologized. Sayid jumped up from the chair beside her. "Sayid wanted to be here when I told everyone."

The waiter brought me an extra chair and I squeezed in beside Miles. Greer looked away without her usual. Maybe Miles had begun cleaning up his own mess after all.

I glanced around, trying to get a sense of the mood. Amy was sniffing and dabbing at her eyes with her napkin, but Gillian looking like she couldn't contain her glee. "What's going on?"

"We're getting married!" Alicia exclaimed.

"That's amazing!" I pushed my chair back to congratulate her with a hug when her next word stopped me in my tracks.

"Tomorrow!"

20

Day Six - At Sea

THE NEXT MORNING, I slept late. We had celebrated Alicia's engagement long into the night. It might have been love at first sight, but it sounded real to me. The legend of Aphrodite had scored another win.

But not for me. When I finally awoke, my unhappiness peered through the pounding headache to remind me today was my last chance to make things right with Will.

At first I thought the knock on the door was part of my headache, but then I heard it again, and louder.

Will.

I stumbled out of the fog of sleep, my confusion mixing with eagerness making me trip over every single thing in my path. But finally I reached the door, and yanked it open with a expectant smile, hoping against hope that Will—

Captain James Kellerman was at my door.

"Uh...hi," I said, holding on to the doorknob with a death grip. I pushed the hair out of my face and wished I'd thrown one of the thick robes over the long T-shirt I wore to sleep in. "Can I...help...?" I trailed off, completely at a loss for words.

The captain stood in the doorway with hands tucked behind his back and wearing a stern expression. "I've been informed that you know my niece Petra Van Brereton."

Deny, deny, deny! Or tell him, yes, I know Petra because I met her on the ship. It was a big boat, so maybe I could bluff this out, have Petra unavailable until I could get off in Miami.

I released the door knob and took at step back, tugging at the hem of my shirt. "I do know her," I admitted. "She gave me her ticket."

Captain Kellerman looked grim. "She called last night."

I closed my eyes with relief. Petra had kept her word. Maybe I had a chance after all. "How is she?" I asked, hoping he believed the sincerity in my tone.

A smile cracked the stony façade. "She's very happy."

"I'm glad. She looked happy when I left her." It was safe to breathe again. Maybe I wasn't about to be dragged off to the brig, or tossed overboard with only a lifeboat to get me back to Miami.

"That still doesn't explain why you would agree to impersonate someone to board my ship."

I caught my breath at the question. "Because she asked me to?" I asked hesitantly. "It wasn't exactly impersonating, I didn't mean to do that. I told people who I was, but just borrowed her passport because there wasn't time to change the ticket. It was all very...last minute."

"Who are you?"

"Seraphina Park-Smith." What were the chances that my name would help anything? But I wasn't about to pull out the parent card. I got into this mess on my own, and I would get out of it.

Captain Kellerman nodded his head. He was an imposing man, with his towering height and stoic face. *He* wouldn't have let the Titanic hit the iceberg and for a moment I considered saying so.

"Sir, I apologize for my lack of judgment in the situation," I said, pulling up every ounce of poise I'd inherited from my mother. "I realize using Petra's passport was wrong and I'll accept whatever consequences are fit for my actions."

Captain Kellerman took a step forward. "Have you enjoyed your stay on the *Aphrodite*?" he asked as I moved to the side and gestured him in.

"It's been amazing." Relief made me giddy. "I wasn't in the best place when I met Petra. I had been trying to avoid some...some unsavoury types...and she really helped me out. But these last few days, I—well, I've changed. I managed to get my life back in order. I hadn't talked to my parents in four years until I landed on Grand Cayman and called them. And I've made friends, which is something I hadn't done in years because I've been so busy looking out for me—" I stumbled to a stop when I realize what I was saying. "I'm sorry, I'm rambling. You don't want to know this."

"Actually, it's very interesting. Petra said you were an Uber driver?" He raised a bushy white eyebrow at the question.

"No. My friend—my former friend is. I was borrowing his car."

"You borrowed quite a lot of things."

I dropped my gaze. "Yes, sir."

"Are you going to be continuing this behaviour after you leave the ship?"

"No, sir." I peeked up at him. "I think I've learned my lesson."

He nodded again. I couldn't read his expression. Was I about to be thrown off the ship, or was he going to give me a hug goodbye? "I take it you've made arrangements to deliver Petra's things back to her?"

"I'm dropping everything off as soon as we get into port," I promised.

"I'll take the passport now," he said.

"Of course." I hurried to the bedroom safe my fingers shaking as I punched in the numbers. Once I had Petra's passport in my hand, I felt the first ray of hope and calmed my steps as I returned. "Here you go."

"Are you aware that impersonating someone is a felony crime?"

My heart sank. "I am, yes."

"How did you get past the officer in charge?"

"It's not his fault!" I burst out, more scared for Will then for myself. "I'm really good at pretending—not that I've done it before, but I've been taught about things like that. Not that I'll ever do it again, but it wasn't the officer's fault."

Captain Kellerman tucked the passport into his shirt pocket and nodded one more time. "See that it's not a habit. You're very lucky that we're still in international waters, Miss Park-Smith. Enjoy the remainder of your cruise."

And then he was gone, leaving me sagging against the door with relief.

I found Xander by the pool, his eyes shaded with a pair of women's sunglasses. "Xander!"

"Shh," he said with a wave of his arm. "How can you be so excited this early in the morning."

"Because the captain came to see me and he didn't kick me off."

That perked him up. "Awesome! I called Petra when I was in Cozumel and she said she would talk to her uncle, but I wasn't sure if she really did it."

"She did, so thank you." I leaned down and threw my arms around him. "You saved me."

"I didn't do much."

"You did a lot for someone you don't know."

Xander lowered his glasses as I stood up. "I know you enough. Plus, Miles vouched for you and if Miles says something..." He trailed off with a sheepish shrug.

"I can't believe I didn't figure out what was going on with the two of you."

"We've kept it pretty low-key. And you did have a lot on your mind."

"Yes, but—" Out of the corner of my eye, I saw a figure pause at the railing, looking over at me. "Will!"

I don't know if Will heard me but he turned and walked off.

"Go," Xander ordered. "Talk to me later."

I didn't wait to be asked twice.

"Will, wait," I called after him. It wasn't until he was about to disappear into the stairwell that he stopped. "I'm sorry," I said automatically. "I didn't want to lie to you."

"Then why did you?"

"Because I was afraid of what you'd think of me."

"Do you know what I think of you now?"

"You're angry," I said carefully. "And you think I'm a spoiled brat. I'm not. I *was*, but I'm not anymore. I've changed Will. Since I got on the ship. Since I've met you."

"I don't know any of this because I have no idea who you were or who you are. I thought you were good and kind and fun, but now all I know is that you didn't trust me enough to tell me the truth. And that could have gotten me fired."

"I didn't know you at the start, so how could I have trusted you? You never would have let me on the boat."

"That would have been a good thing." And with that, he turned and hurried down the stairs.

"Don't say that," I whispered after him.

21

A LICIA ASKED ME TO be the photographer for the wedding. Which meant I had a lot to do; a good thing, because if it wasn't for that, I might have hidden in my room and cried myself into a stupor.

Alicia's wedding day began with a brunch at Mount Orynus and several pitchers of mimosas. I had never been the type to use alcohol to dull pain, but that morning I tried my best, stopping only when I realized drunken pictures were not what Alicia would be looking for.

This was Alicia's day. I couldn't let her down.

After brunch, I went to the Pasithea Spa with Alicia, Amy and Gillian. Greer bowed out at the last moment, using her stomach upset as an excuse.

"She's really sick," Gillian assured me as settled ourselves on the massage tables. "So don't think it's because of you."

I didn't think it was me. I thought it was that Greer couldn't bear for Alicia to have the spotlight, but I wasn't about to say anything.

When I was waiting for my rosewater ice facial, I bumped into Heidi and Lily, my pole dancing partners. I had seen them from a distance a few times this week, but never close enough to talk.

"Did you find your true love?" Heidi squealed.

"No." My slumped shoulders said enough and Lily patted my arm with sympathy.

"There's still today," she said encouragingly.

"We did," Heidi admitted.

"I sort of thought you would."

"And I went back to pole dancing three times!"

I was happy for them, despite my own personal sadness. Now that I looked, I noticed quite a few couples had shown up among the groups of singles.

There was a cocktail party at the bow of the boat that afternoon for Sassy Singles; one last attempt for the members to find Mr. or Ms. Right.

I stayed away.

Instead, Amy organized a makeup artist to give Alicia a makeover and the result was breathtakingly beautiful. Alicia was pretty to begin with but after Karen's transformation and Alicia happiness, there was a glow about her that made everyone who saw her smile.

I stopped looking for Will, knowing how busy he would be, realizing his anger might not abate enough for him to listen to more apologies. Instead, I threw my energy into taking beautiful pictures for Alicia's wedding.

Hers wasn't the only ceremony that day. When news got around that Xander was able to officiate a wedding, he had requests from two other couples as well. I ducked away from Alicia and followed him to the ceremonies, snapping pictures of the happy couples.

I ended up with a list of email addresses to send the pictures, four offers of employment, and my own proposal of marriage from a drunken man in a sailor hat who said it was Aphrodite's dream for us to be together.

When I was returning to Alicia to take pictures of her getting ready, a tall woman with braided hair and a camera around her neck stopped me.

"You wouldn't be Petra, would you?"

"No, I'm Siggy, the photographer formerly known as Petra."

She looked confused. "Do you know Will?"

I smiled at the sound of his name. "Yes."

"I'm Marty. He told me a Petra was helping him take pictures. He described you, so I thought you might be her."

"I am, but my name is really Siggy. Long story," I waved away any further explanation. "Nice to meet you."

"I wanted to thank you for helping Will. His pictures were pathetic, but it was really sweet of him to help me out. I don't know what I would have done without him. Or you. *Your* pictures were amazing. He said you're not a professional?"

"Just a hobby."

"Do you want to do it professionally?"

"Well, sure, but—"

"The reason I'm asking is that I'm leaving the *Aphrodite* after the next cruise. They asked me to help find a replacement, and I found you. Would you be interested?"

"Yes!" I had no idea what the job would entail but it would be a job doing what I loved. "But I need to see my parents first."

"No worries. We don't leave again for another two weeks. Will that give you enough time for a visit?" I nodded, for once speechless. "Come see me tomorrow morning before you disembark and I'll fill you in on what you need to know."

"Thanks, Marty," I managed to call after her.

"I have a job!" I squealed under my breath, doing a little happy dance. And not just any job—a job on the same cruise ship as Will. Now I had another weeklong cruise to convince him to forgive me.

The wedding took place at sunset on the top deck at the rear of the ship. It was beautiful, as all wedding are. Xander showed the appropriate mix of gravitas and humor. Sayid wiped both his and Alicia's tears. And I couldn't help but notice Amy smiling at a man watching the service.

With only a few hours to go, it looked like Aphrodite was still working her magic.

The happy couple had made reservations at the wine bar for after the service. I maxed out my sim card and made my excuses, promised to follow everyone on Instagram and Facebook, and said goodnight.

"Siggy, wait!"

I paused at the doorway, looking back at the table of friends celebrating to see that Miles and Xander had followed me.

"You're not getting away that easily," Xander said, pulling me in for a hug.

"I thought the chances of seeing you again were pretty good," I said into his shoulder.

"But you're only going to be home for two weeks," Miles reminded me.

"But I won't be away forever this time."

"Promise?" Miles asked.

I hugged him in response. "I expect to see you *both* at the party I'm sure my mother will be throwing for me."

"Should I bring my sister?" Xander asked with a grin. "You know, she actually thinks we're making this whole thing up?" He gestured to Miles with his thumb. "Just as an excuse for Miles not to marry her."

"You're joking!"

"She's crazy. But you know who's crazy? You, if you don't go after your guy."

"He's not my guy."

"Then why was he at the wedding?" Miles demanded. "I saw him. Staring at *you*, not the lovely bride and groom."

"Really?"

"Really. What does he do around here anyway?"

"Assistant cruise director."

"So he'll be at the talent show. We're heading over soon, but you should go now and fix things."

"I don't know if I can."

"Try. Now." Miles gave me a shove. "Right now."

"You sound like my big brother," I grumbled, backing away.

"If you don't go I'm going to tell him exactly how big an idiot you've been, so go."

I backed away another few steps. "Thank you," I said, my eyes welling up with tears. "Have fun tonight."

"We'll have more fun than you will," Xander said as he took Miles' hand.

I took their advice because I've always taken my big brother's advice. I couldn't wait to see Simon tomorrow and my parents. But I couldn't be happy about seeing them unless I talked to Will first.

The talent show was in the main theatre and I gazed around in dismay at the crowd. Half the ship's passengers must have been in the audience. But then like radar signaling my heart, I turned to the far corner of the lounge and saw Will standing by himself, doing something to the sound system. I snuck around behind him so he didn't know I was there until I started talking.

I didn't even take a moment to think of what I should say. "You have to listen to me because I know you can't leave," I began as Will started with surprise.

"What are you doing here?" he demanded as he whirled around.

"Trying to apologize."

"I don't want an apology," Will said stiffly. "I deserve an explanation."

"You do. And that's what I'll try and give you, if you just give me a chance."

As passengers sang, danced and told really bad jokes on stage, I began with my family and how I met Charles, leading to our wedding and my discovery that he had drained my bank account four days later. I told Will about leaving home in the middle of the night, about New York and Atlanta and finally landing in Miami with no money and too much pride to call my parents.

I told him about Eduardo and the confidence scam I messed up.

I explained how I had been running away when I met Petra and how the tickets to the cruise had been an easy way out.

Will stood silently, his gaze holding mine as I talked. Taking a deep breath, I reached out and touched his arm. "The first time I saw you, that first day, I felt a real connection with you. I think maybe you did too."

He didn't say a word, but I plunged ahead anyway.

"I know it sounds trite and cliché, but it's true. I'm a better person now. When I got on this ship, it was like all the lights went on. Like I'd been living under this huge cloud, and with a huge gush of air, it just blew away." I waved my hands, releasing all my fears to the sea air. "Maybe it was because I was finally in a safe place, or had time to think instead of reacting. I don't know. I do know that I haven't been able to be myself—my real self—for a long time. And it took pretending to be Petra to make me realize that. And meeting you. I know I'm rambling, but need you to know all this. And I need you to know that, whatever happens, I like you. I like you a lot. And it's just as important that I like *me* better because of you. So thank you for that." My voice cracked and I stopped, willing him to say something.

At that moment the audience burst into cheers. I glanced towards the stage as Janey, the pole dancing instructor rushed down the aisle to join a handsome man in impossibly tiny blue shorts. When I looked back at Will, he was staring at me with an unreadable expression in his eyes.

"Will you say something?" I begged.

"I don't like being lied to," he said.

"I won't ever lie to you again. Even if you have spinach in your teeth, I'll tell you."

Will chuckled, which I thought was a good sign so I opened my mouth to continue, only to have him place a finger across my lips.

"I've heard enough," he said heavily.

"To forgive me?" I asked hopefully.

"To understand a bit of your crazy, mixed-up world. I may need further clarification but this is good for now." And then as the music swelled on stage, he reached for me, tucking a hand under my hair. "I've never liked the name Petra," he whispered, his lips a mere breath from mine. "I much prefer Siggy. It's more you."

And as the audience cheered around us, Will's lips met mine.

Hooked on Siggy and Will? Don't drop anchor just yet!

Join my newsletter crew and grab *Only Facebook Friends*—a free short story to give you a taste of what's next.

I Saw Him Standing There is part of the Oceanic Dreams series.

Check out the other books in the series!

Oceanic Dreams Series

Eight fun, heartwarming romantic comedy novellas by Eight amazing rom-com authors!

I Saw Him Standing There—Holly Kerr

Time of My Life—Laura Heffernan

Circle in the Sand—Tracy Krimmer

I Thought it was You—Kirsty McManus

I Will Follow Him—Holly Tierney-Bedord

Take a Chance on Me—Delancey Stewart

Shut Up and Dance With Me—Monique McDonell

The Best of You—Sophie-Leigh Robbins

Acknowlegments

WRITING I Saw Him Standing There has been one of best times of my career because it's the first time I've worked hand-in-hand with other authors.

Thanks to Delancey, who set sail with the idea, and for Laura and Kirsty, who helped me steer the ship. Thanks to Tracy, Monique, Sophie-Leigh and Holly T who came aboard – you really need to read their books.

Thanks as well to Paula and Nita and Kaitie for picking it apart and helping me put it back together, and for my street team who make me so happy when they want to read my books!

And thanks to all my readers. I wouldn't be doing this if it wasn't for you!

READING LIST

Love in Laandia

Royal Rumble
Royal Retelling
Royal Rising
Royal Reluctance
Royal Rebel

Suitor Science

Hating the Chemistry Teacher
Falling for The Suitor
Fraternizing with the Ex
Marrying the Billionaire Best Friend
Loving the Wrong Guy
Finding the One

Don't

Don't Tell Me You Love Me
Don't Want to Be Friends
Don't Stop Me Now
Don't They Know It's Christmas

Love & Alliteration

Perfectly Played
Beautifully Baked
Pleasantly Popped

Charlotte Dodd

The Secret Life of Charlotte Dodd
The Missing Files of Charlotte Dodd
The Best Worst First Date Ever
The Hidden Past of Pippa McGovern
The Last Stand of Charlotte Dodd

Sisters in a Small Town

Coming Home
Hanging On
Stepping Up

Unexpecting
Unexpectingly Happily Ever After

STANDALONES

Cinnamon Rolls and Pumpkin Spice – Coffee Break with the Billionaire

Oceanic Dreams – I Saw Him Standing There

Absinthe Doesn't Make the Heart Grow Fonder